Killer's Cut

(A DI Shona McKenzie Mystery)

Wendy H. Jones

Published by Scott and Lawson

Cover Design by Cathy Helms of Avalon Graphics LLC

ISBN: 978-0-9930677-8-5

DEDICATION

To Cathy Helms, my cover designer, who has displayed both Dundee and the books so well. Thank you Cathy for capturing the mood and working to bring my stories to life in the covers.

ACKNOWLEDGMENTS

I would like to thank the following people who have helped me in so many ways.

Stephanie Black for her tireless work in acting as Beta Reader and proofreader.

Fellow crime author Chris Longmuir, for all her help and support throughout the process of bringing the book to completion.

Karen Wilson of Ginger Snap Images, Dundee for the professional author photographs.

Nathan Gevers for all his hard work and enthusiasm building the website for my books.

Police Scotland for their patience in answering myriad questions about the nuts and bolts of policing. Particular thanks must go to my local police sergeant who has never failed to answer any of my questions with good humour and has supported me in my endeavor.

The members of the Angus Writers Circle for their valuable advice, feedback and support

.

1

Despite the green-eyed man driving the old Mercedes Benz carefully up the steep mountain road, the human leg still rattled around in the boot. Only the light of a low-slung moon, almost dazzling in its brilliance, lighted his way. The narrow road wound through rocky, gorse covered terrain, known only to the spirits of the night. This was a barren, God forsaken wilderness. The sound of Beethoven's Moonlight Sonata accompanied the occupant of the car. It was a soothing backdrop completely at odds with the macabre purpose of this trip.

The music changed tempo as he reached his destination, quickening in time with his adrenaline fuelled heartbeat. He slipped smoothly from the car and stretched muscles stiff from the journey. Opening the boot he removed his grizzly package and well used spade. Leaving the vehicle unlocked he moved into a small copse and searched for the perfect spot. A pile of autumn leaves caught his attention. The spade was used to dig deeply through these and into the rotting undergrowth below. The package was shoved deep inside the cavity and the dirt shovelled back to fill the gap. The leaves once more placed on top. The man turned and left nature to take its course.

Folding himself back in the car he turned the key and continued his journey. The moon was the only witness to his midnight escapade.

2

DI Shona McKenzie's long legs moved in fluid motion as she chased the offender down a long corridor. He looked back and then made a dart to the right and was off down another corridor. She hurtled after him and caught a glimpse of his retreating back as he ran through a door. Bad move as she now had him cornered. As she entered the room she called back over her shoulder, "Roy, this would be a good time to produce that treat you said you had."

Shona was used to chasing killers throughout the highways and byways of Dundee and it's surrounds. However, this criminal was different. The ruffian who had her entire team chasing him, was a Weineramer puppy. Sitting in a corner, all huge eyes and floppy ears, he chewed on the heel of one of Jimmy Choo's most expensive makes of shoe.

Sgt Nina Chakrabarti hobbled in. "What has that little nightmare done to my shoe?"

The dog looked up startled at her sharp tone. He whined and then returned to his plaything.

"Shut up, you're frightening him," said Shona. "If you will wear designer chic to the office what do you expect? You should wear supermarket's best like the rest of us."

"You might head up CID but you're short on fashion sense. Cheap clothes? Not in a million years." Nina was wrestling the shoe away from the puppy. He was not giving up without a fight and was currently winning.

"It's ruined anyway. Leave him be. I'm sure

you've a spare pair somewhere."

Nina, who had a face as grey as the finest Scottish thunderstorm, opened her mouth to reply. She was fortunately interrupted by the arrival of Roy with a dog treat. The Puppy, tail wagging, dropped the shoe and took the proffered treat.

"Why the he... heck have we got a dog in the nick anyway?" asked Nina. She stopped herself from swearing just in time. The DI didn't tolerate swearing. Nina's day was already bad enough without adding a bollocking from the boss.

"It's for auld Jock," said Shona.

At the mention of Jock, Nina calmed right down. "Why didn't you say so? Poor Jock's been miserable without his wee dog. I must say I miss wee Maggie myself."

"I only hope Jock likes him," said Shona.

He would have his work cut out for him. This little chap was a bundle of mischief and fun. Shona slipped the lead back on and led him back to her office. He had a blanket on the floor with a few chewy toys. Shona bent down to fondle his ears. "It serves her right. She shouldn't have taken her shoe off."

The puppy nipped her hand. He then tried to grab *her* shoe.

The phone rang, and, shoving the dog away with one hand, Shona picked it up.

"Shona it's Gordon Bessant, from the Highlands and Islands. We've something here I thought might interest you."

"If you think you need my help I would take a wild guess it's a dead body."

"It is, well almost."

"How can you almost have a dead body? It's either dead or it isn't. I'm sure the local police surgeon would be able to help you out on that front."

"Very witty. The daughter of one of our sergeants has found a leg buried in a copse not far off the A83 near Inveraray."

"How old is this kid if she's allowed to traipse around a wood looking for body parts?"

"She's not a kid. She's twenty-two and about to go to Sandhurst to do her officer training. She was out running and had her dad's dog with her. It's an ex police dog so started rooting around."

"Why do you need my help? You're a long way from my patch."

"You're Scotland's go to girl for the weird and wonderful."

"Yeah right. Shona Mckenzie superhero." Shona's reputation for collecting strange cases had her dragged into all sorts.

"I'll send you through some photos."

"Is that leg real? You're not yanking our chains are you?" said Roy McGregor one of Shona's DC's. "It's a bit late for April fool jokes."

"Roy your use of language never ceases to amaze me. Of course I'm not 'yanking your chain' as you so delicately put it."

"Why would anyone wrap a human leg in brown paper and tie it up with a lump of string?" asked Nina Chakrabarti. "Then bury it?" she added.

Shona had three sergeants in her department and Nina was one of them.

"How the frig do I know, Nina. I'm a detective not a soothsayer. It's our job to find out, not make wild guesses."

They were looking at some perfect photographs blown up and displayed in all their glorious technicolour glory. They could almost feel they were inside the trees looking down at the crime scene. The edges of the wound appeared neat. It seemed like a saw had been used to separate the leg from the torso.

"Are we going to go and have a look, Ma'am? I'd love to get my hands on that crime scene." DC Iain Barrow was never happier than when paddling around in fingerprints and swabs.

"Hold your horses cowboy. I haven't made a decision yet. I'm not sure there's anything we could add that the local force haven't already done."

"But they've asked for our help."

"Stop begging Iain. By the time we get up there much of the evidence may have deteriorated. We can't go gallivanting about the countryside until we're sure it's our case."

"Even I've worked out it's usually our case. A jaunt to the Highlands and Islands would be nice. I could catch up with my mates." Abigail had joined them from The Isle of Skye a couple of years ago.

"I'll think about it."

Asking the chief's advice was probably one of Shona's more stupid moves.

"You are not travelling half way across Scotland on a whim. Let them do their own work."

"Sir, we're police Scotland now. We go where we're needed."

"Don't you think I know that McKenzie. I'm sure even you can work out you're not needed. Advise them from a distance."

"Of course Sir. Thank you for your advice." She left, harbouring murderous thoughts of chopping him up and depositing him in a remote spot. This cheered her up considerably and gave her more fodder for the book she was writing - *DI Shona McKenzie's Guide to Killing your Boss*.

The team were not happy with their incarceration.

"I'm sure we could help somehow."

"Stop whining, Soldier Boy," said Shona. "Tell me you didn't act like this in Afghanistan." DC Jason Roberts had joined the police straight from a tour with the TA.

"He's right. I'm bored. We haven't had a decent case in months," said Roy.

"You pair agreeing. That has to be a first. Suck it up and stop acting a like a couple of brats. If you want to help the Highlands and Islands then go and do some searching on HOLMES or the net."

"If I look up body parts dot com I'll probably get some hits," says Roy.

"That's enough Roy. This isn't funny."

A strangled sound came from Nina's direction. She was trying not to laugh. Shona threw her a dirty look and walked from the office.

Shona had to agree with the team. She was fed up being stuck inside as well. Bell Street station closely resembled the Gulags. In recent years they'd tarted up the insides but the outside still left a lot to be desired. Shona was sitting at her pristine desk wishing she had a few cases to clutter it up. Not that she was champing at the bit to go out to a crime scene. Her last case had shaken her nerve somewhat. The long gap between cases was not helping to throw this feeling off. She picked up the phone and broke the news to Gordon that she wouldn't be joining him.

"I'm surprised. I thought you'd jump at the chance for a trip up North."

"The chief is blowing a gasket about CID's petrol bill. He says our operating costs are twice the size of any other department."

"I hear you. I get the same thing."

"We'll do what we can from here to take the pressure of your guys a bit." With that she hung up.

In usual Shona fashion she didn't have long to wait before her phone rang again. "Ma'am, it's the desk sergeant. I've a young lad here who wants to speak to a copper. Sounds like it's you he needs. I've sent some uniform to the scene to start the process."

"What's he after?"

"You'd be better hearing it from him."

"Bring him to my office."

She sighed. Here we go again. Despite the fact she might be starting a new case, her stomach tightened. "No. I will not be nervous. Shove off," she said to the empty office. Empty apart from the puppy. It whined at her tone. "Sorry, Pup." The animal wriggled as she tickled his tummy. I wish I were as easily soothed she thought.

The young lad was only about twelve years old. He was covered in mud from head to toe. Tears had washed some of the worst of it from his face. His name was Damien.

"Your mum or dad will need to be here when we talk to you. What's their number?" asked Shona.

The phone call made, Abigail took the boy off to find some cake or a biscuit. The station was usually awash with such delicacies. She held his muddy hand rather loosely. His father took about ten minutes to get there.

"What's the little brat done now? I try to keep him out o' bother but he just ignores me."

"Mr Lawrence, he's not done anything. He found something and I need to speak to him."

Moving into an interview room, Shona asked the boy what he saw.

His lip trembled and he said. "It was a hand. Sticking out the ground. It was horrible." He burst into tears.

"Why were you no' at school? You'll get me in bother."

"Mr Lawrence." Shona's tone is sharp. "You can worry about that later."

She turned back to Damien. "Where did you see the hand?"

"Sticking out the ground. I said that already."

"Damien, dinnae be cheeky or I'll tan yer a..."

"Mr Lawrence. Please?" Shona's tone left no room for a repeat of the misdemeanour. She turned to the boy. "I meant where in Dundee?"

"Up the Law Hill." The hill part was redundant as everyone in Dundee and its surrounds knew Law meant hill in old Scottish. However, most people still used the full title. There was less room for confusion that way.

"Right you lot, we're off on a jaunt." Everyone looked up.

"Up North?" asked Iain as he stood and moved.

"Take it easy, Flash. We're going for an outing up the law. Looks like there could be a dead body."

Their faces alight with eagerness they reached for their coats.

"That's the ticket, Ma'am," said Peter. That summed it up for them all. The lack of a meaty case to chew on had been getting them all down.

3

The powerful purr of a well maintained engine was the only sound as the car climbed steadily up the precipitous hill. Darkness engulfed the vehicle despite the bright lights of the city far below. Gloomy cloud obliterated any glimmer of moonlight. This was a dark, lonely sojourn for the car's occupant. He was accompanied only by his thoughts. They were focussed on what lay ahead.

He stepped from the car and opened the boot. Inside lay only three things - a plastic sheet, a pick axe and a human arm wrapped in brown paper. Grabbing the latter two he climbed carefully into the undergrowth. Once deep inside, hidden by a thick canopy of Scottish fir trees, he placed the package carefully on the ground. He gripped the handle of the pick axe and raised it above his head. A muffled thunk as the undergrowth and solid ground gave way. Thunk, thunk, thunk. No one to hear. No one to see. Seven minutes later the package was buried, the earth and undergrowth replaced. Not one earthly soul would visit this spot.

His job done, he and the car wound their way back down the road towards the city lights.

4

The law, an extinct volcano, dominated the city skyline. Shona drove up the winding road past a vast sentinel of tall Scots for trees. The heavy rain of the past few days had given way to bright sunshine. Raindrops glimmered in the branches lending a peaceful air to the area. Things weren't quite so peaceful at the crime scene. Sergeant Muir the Police Official Licensed Search Advisor, or POLSA stopped them. They were nowhere near the crime scene.

"What's up?" asked Shona.

"The place is a mudbath, Ma'am. There's been a mudslide. That's probably what unearthed the hand."

Ah! That would explain Damian's appearance.

"That's all we need. Who's up there?"

"No one at the moment. We wanted you to see it before muddy boots caused havoc."

"Thanks. You're a good man Sergeant Muir."

"You'll be ruining my reputation, Ma'am."

She went to speak to Peter. "This is a mare. Our footprints are going to be all over it like branding."

"Aye. Might be better to get Iain to take as many photos as he can. He could use one o' those long lenses he's so fond of."

"I'd already thought of that Watson." She paused, then, "Only Iain and I will go in. We'll get full gear on."

The long-range photos taken, Shona and Iain, suited head to toe in white, looked like a pair of ghosts. They trod like cats and looked for evidence at every

10

step.

"Those small footsteps are probably Damien's," said Iain.

"I'd put a couple of bob on you being right. Get photos and casts. I'll help."

Cataloguing everything they made their way towards the appendage. Damien was right; it seemed to be waving hello from the grave. Progress was painfully slow as they took care not to damage any existing prints. Not that they were expecting any. Mudslides were not a great respecter of evidence. At last they reached it and took in the scene. There was indeed a muddy hand, which appeared human, peeking from the ground. The hand was also partially decomposed.

"Why isn't Mary here?" Shona pulled her iPhone from her pocket and called Peter. Mary was the pathologist for Dundee.

"She's on her way, Ma'am. The POLSA thought you'd be asking. She was just finishing off an autopsy."

Shona stood stock-still and cast a beady eye around the scene. A tree had been uprooted in the slide. It's roots reached into the sky, like brown bones dripping muddy blood, searching for eternal rest in the heavens above. They lent an eerie backdrop to the scene. Shona shivered. "Get a grip woman," she muttered.

"What was that, Ma'am?" Iain appeared from around the tree.

"Nothing. Just thinking aloud." No way would Shona show her fear to any member of her team.

"Have you found anything?" she asked.

"Some footsteps. I've taken cracking photos. Put a tripod up to get it at the right angle. I'll be doing casts." Iain may have been short on words but he was big on collecting evidence. No stone left unturned as the saying went.

Shona heard the squelching of Mary's covered

wellies long before she saw her.

"You've never had me out at one of your scenes yet, Shona. Fancied some company did you?"

"This one's decomposing and buried in mud. Expert advice is needed."

"I do like a puzzle. This is going to take me more than five minutes." She stared at the terrain and the mud covered arm.

"If that's a whole body then it'll take you a lot longer than that. However, the Highlands and Islands have discovered a leg—"

"A leg? So your saying this could be just an arm."

"Yeah. Or maybe a body missing a leg." She pauses. "Maybe it's nothing to do with their leg."

"Just when I think your cases couldn't get any more strange, you surprise me."

"Could you look for some brown wrapping paper and string?"

"If there's even a morsel to be found then it will have your name on it. Joking apart, most of this muck will be going to your lab. I'm sure there will be enough in it to keep the crime lab boys happy for a decade."

"That's what I was afraid of."

Shona returned to her team who all had faces like the back end of a bus.

"What are we doing here?" asks Nina.

"All this hanging about is no' good for my feet," says Peter.

"If there were Oscars for whinging, you lot would win uncontested. Why are you hanging about anyway? You should be looking for evidence. Shoo."

They trudged off, still complaining.

It wasn't long before Mary was back to speak to Shona. "I can confirm that there's an arm and nothing else. Not in that spot anyway. We're going to have to check for any other body parts around the area. It looks like the Law's going to be out of commission for a while."

"The natives will like that. We've already got a load of gawkers. Fine upstanding citizens who are supposedly walking their dogs. I'll move them on."

Mary turned to tramp back up the hill and Shona turned to the onlookers. "Right you lot, we're expanding the crime scene. I need you to move right back to the bottom of the hill."

"This is a public place. I've a right to walk my dog here."

"My badge says my crime scene trumps your right to amble about the law. Now you and your dog trot off or I'll arrest you both."

"You can't talk to me like that."

"I just did. Now, I won't say it again. Move."

They were all moved on, helped by the uniformed officers who were now placing the crime scene tape further down the hill. Shona could hear the sound of, "Trust the pigs. Using their power when there's nae need."

"That told them, Ma'am. You're in fine fettle."

"What are you doing back here, Peter?"

"I've organised the others and thought you might need a hand."

She updated him on the situation and said, "We need to get dogs and search the whole area."

"Would you like me to sort that out for you?"

"Fill your boots. I'm off back up to see Mary."

"Leave me to do all the hard work, eh Ma'am."

"Hard work. All you've got to do is whip a high tech phone from your pocket and make a phone call. If you think that's hard work, you need to retire."

"Have you met the station dogs? They're a wild bunch."

"Stop moaning and get on with it. Surely a few wee

13

puppies aren't going to worry you."

Mary was appreciative of the dogs but asked if they could be held off from the immediate area for the moment. The answer was, of course, yes. Mary was the foremost pathologist in the country and Shona would do anything to help her do her job. Mary, on the other hand, would say Shona mainly gave her all her work. Without Shona's ability to attract dead bodies the mortuary would be a very quiet place. The arm was now displayed and looking decidedly moth eaten, or maggot eaten as the case may be. There were also a number of flies as was usual where decaying flesh is involved.

"How can you work with all that buzzing going on around your head? What a racket," said Shona.

"I'm a bit Mutt and Jeff but mostly I just ignore it."

"That's pretty impressive. Any other body parts appeared nearby?"

"Not yet. I've been concentrating on this area for the minute. Once I've got it squared away we can widen the area."

"I feel like an archaeologist."

"I'm not sure why. I'm doing all the work." Mary's smile took the sting from her words.

"Good point. What can I do?"

Mary handed Shona a small spade and pointed her in the direction of a pile of mud.

"Get digging. You're looking for that paper and string you're so keen to find. Be gentle." Mary handed her a soft brush. "Use this as well."

They carried on with their grizzly task whilst Iain took photographs.

"Are you entering these photos into a competition in Photographers Monthly, or something?" asked Shona. "Take some photos of the surroundings and leave us alone. I feel like a supermodel."

"I am taking photos of the scene. You pair just happen to be in the way."

"Oh, forgive me if we're ruining the crime scene for you! Would you like us to leave?" There was enough sarcasm dripping from Shona's voice that it could have been used to paint the dry stane dyke that sat just above them. "Don't be so beggaring cheeky."

"It's a laugh a minute working with you lot," Mary said between gales of laughter. "Are you always like this."

Shona was prevented from answering by the sounds of barking. The cavalry had arrived in the form of the dogs.

Shona placed her spade and brush carefully on the ground. "I'm off to calm this lot down." She headed down the hill.

The dogs, supposedly highly trained, were acting like they were rabid.

"What a frigging noise. Can't you lot keep these beasts under control?" Her bellow, muffled by the barking, was whipped out of her mouth by the wind. It tossed her words into the air and belted them in the direction of Aberdeen. Not a soul responded to her question.

"Peter, get this shambles sorted out," she shouted into his ear. "This is a crime scene not a kennels."

The others, alerted by the uproar, hurtled down a path and catapulted onto the road. This set the dogs barking even more loudly. Straining at their leashes they lunged towards the newcomers. Jason jumped back and tripped over Roy. He fell and let out a cry of pain as he thumped down on his hand.

"You have got to be kidding me. You must be the clumsiest copper in the history of policing." Despite her sharp tone Shona pulled Jason up by his uninjured arm.

She peered at his hand.

"Nina, you're our resident first aider. Does soft lad here need to go up to A&E?"

Nina threaded her way through the dogs and examined his hand. "Nah. It seems okay." She let go of his hand. "It's probably just shock you wee sook," she said to Jason.

He'd got over his shock rather quickly as he grinned at her.

"Keep an eye on it. If it starts swelling then you've a trip to Ninewells Hospital in your future," said Shona.

"I'll be fine, Ma'am. I had worse than this in Afghanistan."

"You know what, I think the Army were delighted to be rid of you. Their bill for accident reports has probably gone down. Ours on the other hand..." She didn't even have the energy to finish the sentence.

"I'll fill one out when I get back to the station."

Despite the mayhem they managed to get the dogs under control. Once they were separated the dogs calmed down, and the search was efficient. It took several hours but turned up nothing. There wasn't another body part to be found.

Shona drove back to the concrete monstrosity called Bell Street station.

Standing proudly just off the centre of town, the sight of it always made Shona miserable. In days long gone prisoners had been hanged just outside. They'd even had a hanging in the station. The inside was better these days given it had had a makeover. Despite the wishes of most of the inmates, both prisoners and staff, there was nothing that could be done about the outside. Short of blowing it up, of course, but Shona thought that was taking it too far. They would probably end up working from the hall in the church up the road. That was worse than the station. At least the station was dry. The same could not be said of the church of the leaky roof.

5

Once back in her office, Shona grabbed a mug of the sludge the station called coffee and slugged it down. Several hours on the side of a windswept mountain had not done anything for her heat levels. She was frozen to the gills and beyond. Also, the coffee served as a restorative before facing the chief.

A couple of minutes and a succinct explanation later the chief was up to speed. Shona waited for the inevitable explosion. She was not disappointed.

"I take it you're using this as an excuse to drive up North."

"It's not an excuse, Sir. We really do need to go."

"Can you not have a day without causing havoc and costing me a fortune?"

Shona felt that silence was the best course of action. Saying sorry would only have made things worse.

"I suppose you'd better go. Take one member of your team. If the others are not gainfully employed I'll find something for them to do."

"We'll need to stay in a hotel overnight."

"Why does that not surprise me? Make sure it's a cheap one."

"Thank you, Sir."

Shona left the office wondering if she could feed the chief's chopped up body to the resident dog pack. Mind you she would probably poison the dogs and would have animal rights activists on her tail as well.

Maybe not then, she thought. She rather liked the station pack despite their ability to clutter up a crime scene.

"Peter, you're coming with me. We're off to visit the boys in blue up in the Highlands and Islands. We need to get up close and personal with their crime scene."

"What about the rest of us?" asked Abigail.

"You lot are going to be up close and personal with a pile of dirt. Iain, you're in charge. Noses to the grindstone. The chief's on the warpath."

Nina opened her mouth to speak. Shona cut her off before she could utter one syllable.

"I couldn't care less about your designer clothes. I'm sure you'll find something in the box we keep for vagrants."

Nina shuddered. "I'm sure I'll work something out."

"Glad to hear it. Now, hop to it. Iain why is everyone still sitting around."

There was a general melee and the team trooped off after Iain.

Shona headed towards her office to grab her coat and bag. She found the dog chewing on a kidskin leather glove. She had no clue as to its owner. Given its size she suspected it belonged to a woman. She fired off a quick email to everyone on the station email list. It said if they'd lost a glove, to stop looking. She also advised them that buying a new pair might be in order.

"Fagin, you'll be the death of me."

The dog jumped up and licked her hand.

"You like that name do you?"

The dog wagged his tail.

"Fagin it is then. Come on, we're off on a wee outing." She grabbed his lead and the excited puppy pranced alongside her. There was nothing like the thought of a trip to keep your spirits up. Especially when the firm was paying for it.

She sent Peter home to grab an overnight case and told him to pick her up at her flat. He could drive.

6

"Where is Inveraray, Peter? I've never even heard of it."

"It's a town at the other side of Loch Fyne."

"Which is where?"

"On the west coast about three hours away. Can we stop to get something to eat? We're missing our tea."

"For goodness sake, Peter. Let's get there before we worry about dinner. I can't run my investigation according to the whims of your stomach."

The journey continued in silence apart from Radio 4 blasting from the speakers.

The dog was lying peacefully on a blanket in the boot of the car. He was guarding a stuffed monkey.

The discussion about food was a moot point, as they were driving along roads which became increasingly narrower and more rural. There was nowhere open en route. Even Shona was beginning to think her throat had been cut. Their journey took longer as they got stuck behind a herd of cows.

"What is it with animals. I can't seem to move for them today."

"Just think yourself lucky that it's no' George Broon and thon Russians."

"Jeez, Peter. Pa Broon and the Alexeyev twins. I've enough problems without the Ex Lord Provost and a brace of Russian thugs."

"I'm sure they'll turn up soon enough. They're probably waiting for us in Inveraray."

"Peter. That's not funny."

"I wasn't trying to be funny."

A gloomy silence descended as they drove the final leg. Inveraray appeared shut up as tight as a misers purse.

They were both thankful that the hotel looked bright and cheery. Shona hadn't gone too downmarket and the hotel had an excellent restaurant. It was ruined by a couple of bolshie women. One of them was complaining.

"They're sat at our table. We've been at that table all week."

Shona's trigger finger was twitching. "Can we arrest them?"

"I'm sure we could if we tried hard enough."

Fortunately for the women, Shona and Peter's food arrived.

Steak, chips, a large Talisker Whisky and a couple of pints of Tenants soon had them feeling much more on top of their game. The chef even provided Fagin with some scraps and allowed him into the almost empty dining room. That might be because Shona informed them he was a police dog in training. There was no use in letting the truth interfere with a good story. Besides, it was almost true. He would be Bell Street's adopted mascot.

"I'm almost glad we had this wee journey. It was worth it just to land here," said Peter.

"I couldn't agree more."

"Will the procurator fiscal and his bairns no' be missing you?"

"I'm sure they're devastated. I'm off to ring them and put them out of their misery."

Douglas Lawson, the procurator fiscal, was Shona's boyfriend. He was probably out of his mind thinking she'd disappeared again. She wasn't too worried as the station would have given him her whereabouts.

There wasn't a strong signal in wilds of nowhere, Scotland. In fact, there was no signal. It looked like she'd be using the hotel phone. She'd chalk it up to expenses.

Back in her room she kicked off her shoes, flopped onto the king sized bed and picked up the phone. She was accompanied by a large glass of whisky and an exhausted Fagin. The dog decided Shona's bed was the most comfortable spot in the room and curled up with his stuffed monkey. Shona hadn't the heart to lob him off. She'd grown quite fond of the wee thief. He'd actually stolen the monkey from somewhere. Shona decided it was a waste of manpower investigating the theft.

The next morning broke grey and dull but dry. Having spent many an hour in amongst dripping trees, Shona was eternally grateful for the lack of the wet stuff. She was also grateful that she'd had a decent nights sleep and a gargantuan breakfast. The view as they drove was stunning. Mist enshrouded mountains bordered moody lakes.

"It's a scene just begging for a murder," said Shona.

"It's a wonder the body part was found given this wilderness," said Peter.

"Maybe it's why there are so many crime books set in Scotland."

"Yon writers certainly have a lot to work with."

They picked their way carefully up the steep mountainside. Littered with rocks and coarse tufts of undergrowth it was a trap for weak ankles. Treading carefully, Shona sent up a prayer of thanks that Jason wasn't involved. The large tent covering the crime scene billowed in the wind. This was despite the shelter of the trees. A large number of white clad police officers were streaming in and out. At least Shona assumed they were police officers. They could have been the tea lady for all she knew. One of them strode up to her. He held out his gloved hand.

"Hi Shona, good to see you."

Shona surmised this was Gordon. "You too. Have you somewhere we can get kitted out and take a look?" She waved Peter over. "Have you met my sergeant?"

"Aye, we've met," said Peter. "About fifteen years ago. We were working on a Scotland wide drugs bust."

"I'll never forget it," said Gordon. "We had some fun."

Much as Shona wanted the finer details, they didn't have time. She dragged Peter off. They returned fully suited and booted and ready to find body parts.

As they entered the tent, Gordon introduced them to the local Pathologist.'

"Ah. The infamous Shona McKenzie." He had a soft Scottish lilt. "Mary's been telling me all about you."

"I bet she has. Is it okay for us to look around?"

He indicated it was and turned back to his duties.

The leg had been removed, and was probably occupying a drawer in the mortuary. Countless personnel carefully combed the area. The repeated flash of a camera bounced off the white overalls, giving it the look of a film set. Despite the bustle, all was calm. Peter was busy chatting with one of his muckers.

"Any chance you might join me, Peter?" said Shona.

"I've no' seen him for about ten years."

"You'll not see him again if you don't help. You'll be joining the body parts."

"I'm at your service. What can I do, Ma'am?"

"Get an update from your contemporary. On the crime scene, not his social life."

"Aye." He wandered off.

Shona turned to Gordon. "Anything to go on?"

"Nothing at the moment. It's been battering with rain for days. We've no clue how long the leg's been there either."

"It's a bit odd that there are no other body parts. The two we've got have to be connected."

"I'd agree. I think the next step is DNA testing. If they're a match we have ourselves a puzzle."

"If they don't connect we have ourselves an even bigger puzzle."

"Only you Shona. Only you. I never thought I'd be dragged into one of your hair brained cases."

"How come this is my case all of a sudden?"

"They're always your cases, Shona. We're handing it over to you to head up the MIT team."

"Yeah. Another outlandish case." Despite her jocular tone Shona's mind was racing. Was there a connection? Why were body parts turning up in woods? Did they have another serial killer on their hands? In the words of Sherlock Holmes, the case was afoot. In this instance the case was literally a foot.

The leg looked unnatural under the harsh mortuary lights. This, and the fact it lay in isolation detached from the remainder of the body.

"It's not been buried long." The pathologist pointed to a few small areas of disintegration. "There's not been time for it to decay."

"Approximate time frame?"

"Difficult to say without looking more closely. I've got an entomologist on board. He's as expert as you get."

Shona sighed.

"It's no use making wild guesses lassie. You'll want a proper fix on this."

"You're right. Sorry."

Shona moved closer to the leg. She pulled a photo from her bag and compared them.

"The skin tone does look like the arm we've got in custody." She turned to the pathologist. "Looks like a female leg to me. What's your take?"

"I agree. A fit younger female at that."

"Can I take more photos?"

"I can't see any harm. You're the police after all."

Shona whipped out her iPhone and snapped off a few shots.

"Thanks. Could we have some DNA?"

The pathologist obliged. The sample handed over, she and Peter strode off to find Gordon.

Gordon had returned from the crime scene and provided both coffee and a seat. Shona sank onto the hard chair like it was the finest leather sofa. Peter thudded into the one next to her and stretched out his legs.

"All this wandering about on hillsides is no' good for my feet."

"I see you're still moaning fit to bust?" said Gordon

Shona, used to Peter's moaning, ignored him.

"I think we need to work together on this one. I'll head it up as you asked. It's too strange to be a coincidence."

"Right you are. Keep me posted. Anything you need just ask," said Gordon

They drank their tea and departed for Dundee. Little did they know where else this case was going to take them?

7

How did one dispose of a body? This was something which had occupied his thoughts for many years. In fact let's take one step back. How did one kill another person in the first place? He spent many hours researching and thinking about these points. This was long before information could be found at the click of a button on a computer keyboard. Long before the Internet existed. Thoughts such as these filled his every waking moment. Fascinated by the delicate balance between life and death. Whilst the thoughts of other children his age turned to bikes, dolls and other toys, his brain cells were occupied with much more macabre thoughts. Yes, he could pass himself off in any situation. He was not the awkward outsider of horror books. But he kept his deepest thoughts to himself. Gave little of himself away. If he gave his thoughts away they would lock him up. Out on a bike ride with his mates, most boys of his age were not plotting how he could kill the others. Steep roads edging sheer drops gave him plenty of ammunition. One shove and Jimmy would be over. No chance of surviving that. He, tearful, would tell how a fox darted in front of the bike. Jimmy swerved and there was nothing he could do to stop it.

On the other hand that was a little too impersonal. Battering Jimmy over the head and burying him under some sturdy Scottish rocks sounded better. He would see the fear in his victim's face. He could then say they had a fight and Jimmy went off on his own. The only flaw in this was his clothes. They would be covered in blood. Even his batty mother might notice that and find it strange. This one might need to be thought out more carefully. However, it did give him something to work with.

All the time he was thinking this he would chatter and smile. Friends out for a bike ride with no sign of the evil undercurrent. Plus Jimmy was a prize winning boxer. One punch from the volatile Jimmy and the death might be his own. He needed a much more pliable victim. No, make that victims. He wouldn't stop at one. This thought made him smile even more brightly.

As he matured this obsession grew. The adult library gave him rich pickings. Books on forensic science were devoured. His brilliant brain took note of every sentence, every word, and even every punctuation mark. The habits and nuances of serial killers were as normal to him as breathing. Their names were sweeter than honey to him. This was his life, his very reason for being. There was one difference between him and the other serial killers. He would not get caught. He would make certain of that.

Yet he still did not know how to commit the perfect crime. Nor had he answered the question - how does one dispose of a body? But the answer would come. One day the answer would come.

8

As they drove towards the city, mist crept in. At first a mere wisp, as ethereal as a ghost, drifted past the window. Then it caressed the tops of the trees with gentle, sensitive tendrils. Dundee welcomed them back with fog as thick as a polar bears fur. This was fog that meant business and made their business harder.

"The weather here never ceases to amaze me. I'm just waiting for a typhoon or a hurricane."

"We dinnae get them here, Ma'am."

"No? You do surprise me. How about a whirlwind, or a dust storm? Surely you must get those. Are there any weather conditions I've missed?"

Peter wasn't sure what the best answer was so kept quiet. He concentrated on the job of getting them safely back to the station.

The team welcomed them back to their bosoms.

"Blimey, we've only been gone a couple of days. You can't have had time to miss us?" said Shona.

"The chief's run us ragged. We're knackered," said Nina.

"I thought you were a slave driver, but you're not a patch on that old ba… besom."

"Roy. That's quite enough. If I hear you talk about the chief like that again you'll be receiving your P45." Shona was trying to keep her face straight. There was nothing like a couple of days of the chief to make them appreciate her.

"We've brought you some home made tablet. That

might make you feel a wee bit better," said Peter.

"All righty," said Roy as he grabbed the bag.

"Sugar, butter, condensed milk and dripping with calories. Just what we need," added Morag.

The Scottish confectionary was obviously hitting the spot.

The team fell on it hungrily and soon forgot their woes. It is amazing what a million calories worth of pure indulgence can do for morale.

"Inspector, is it too much to ask that you come and update me on the progress of the case. Why is it that I have to come and find you?"

"Sorry, Sir. I–"

"Never mind making excuses. I am in charge of this station. I am to be updated on any future developments immediately. Are you receiving me loud and clear."

"Yes, Sir. Sorry Sir." Three bags full, Sir. She gave the chief a succinct overview of their case so far.

"Now I will be able to give the chief superintendent the information he has requested."

Ah. That explains the chief's bad mood, thought Shona. "I'll make sure—"

She was talking to the chief's retreating back. She had a feeling she would like to see the three bags she was thinking about earlier stuffed with the chief's body parts. That would cheer her up considerably.

Feeling antsy she decided she needed another look at the crime scene on the Law. Grabbing her keys she barrelled down the corridor.

"I'll be back soon," she yelled through the squad room door as she whizzed past.

She got as far as the main door of the station and stopped fast. She wasn't going anywhere in this. The spectral glow of the streetlights was doing a poor job of lighting Dundee. Enveloped in an ever-deepening fog, the light fractured and spread in a million directions. Not one of these directions was the road. Jack the ripper would have struggled to carry out his duties in this. Despite her reputation as a rally driver, Shona wasn't taking any unnecessary risks. She sighed and turned back through the doorway.

What was it with Dundee and weather? The city seemed to have twenty million varieties of it, and they all came in the one day.

A cup of dark Brazilian blend coffee and a couple of stickie buns cheered her up.

She turned to the mountain of paperwork. Picking up the first one her good mood plummeted. It was a report on the crime rates in Scotland by district. It would appear Dundee had the highest crime rate in the nation. This was 67% higher than the rest of Scotland. On the bright side, the solve rate in her department was 93.2%, much higher than the average. She picked up the next one and started reading. Movement of the paper startled her. Then it moved again. Fagin was trying to pull it from her hands.

"Leave off Fagin. This is important police documentation. You'll be put in jail for stealing it."

Unperturbed the puppy continued to pull and a tug of war ensued. The paper tore and a triumphant puppy bore his spoils of war back to his blanket. He gazed longingly at it. Shona seized her moment and grabbed the paper. Chocolate brown eyes turned towards her, pleading mirrored in their deep pools. Her heart melted but she remained stoic.

"Not a chance mister."

The puppy's tail wagged and Shona had to smile. Lobbing both parts of the report at the bin she sat down.

She was sure the contents would have had her weeping in to her coffee anyway. From the corner of her eye she could see the puppy eyeing up the bin. His brain was planning the next attack.

"One move towards that and you're on next year's barbecue."

The puppy jumped up and licked her hand. The little thief would be free to live another day. The ringing phone sealed the deal.

9

How did she know it would be the duty sergeant with another tale of doom, gloom and dead bodies? Well, body parts actually. One part in particular. Another leg.

"Where is it this time, Sergeant? Sweden? Norway? Cornwall?"

"You're fine, Ma'am. No need to travel far. It's in Baxter Park."

"That place seems to feature a lot in my investigations. It's like the murder capital of Dundee."

The park may only have been 15 minutes away but in this weather it would take at least forty-five minutes, and that was a conservative estimate. Blue lights were useless as they faded into the deepening fog. The sirens were also muffled and gave no indication of direction to other road users. Shona had to console herself with peering through the windscreen and drumming her fingers on the steering wheel.

Baxter Park was situated half way up the Arbroath Road. It was usually a pleasant oasis in the midst of the hustle and bustle of the busy main road. Designed by Sir Joseph Paxton, it also contains a stunning 19th Century Pavilion. The park and pavilion were gifted to the people of Dundee in 1863, as a place of rest and relaxation. This was not the way Shona would describe it now. Cordoned off by the police, a crowd had gathered and were vociferous in their protests.

The young policeman on the gate was struggling to shut them up.

"You lot. Move away from the crime scene tape."

"We have a right to be in that Park," shouted one brave soul. The rest had calmed down and remained quiet.

"And I have a right to arrest every last one of you."

"You can't talk to us like that."

"That's funny I could swear I just did. Now move, or I'm calling for vans to cart you off." She whipped out her iPhone and started dialling.

The still stroppy crowd dispersed. A couple of dog walkers lingered.

"Anything I can help you with?" asked Shona.

One of them obviously didn't hear the sarcastic edge to Shona's voice as he said, "I was hoping I could help you. Boxer here," he indicated the dog, "is a trained search and rescue dog. We're used to searching for body parts in disaster areas."

"That's kind of you. Stay there and if we need you we'll give a yell." Shona didn't even have the energy to find out how he knew about the body parts. She'd learned that bad news travels fast. Whoever found the leg was probably his pal. Worst case scenario, he'd read it on Twitter.

Somehow they managed to find their way up the hill to the relevant area. They could have done with using boxer to guide them. Once they arrived they were no better off.

"How the blazes did they ever investigate the Ripper Murders in weather like this?" asked Shona.

"I cannae even see my hands never mind someone else's body parts," was Peter's helpful contribution.

"We'll just have to get up close and personal with the part in question."

"I'm no' sure my knees will let me. They're playing up in this damp."

"Peter, you're a right crock. If you weren't so

knowledgeable I'd kick you out." There was humour in Shona's voice. She wouldn't part with Peter for any reason. Peter knew it.

"Jason. Iain. You're on. I need you to get down and dirty with the crime scene."

The boys obliged and all three of them peered at the leg.

"Well, I can tell you at a glance that this does not match either of the two other body parts," said Shona

"I think you just might be right," added Iain.

Despite being badly decomposed it was easy to see that the leg belonged to someone who was not Caucasian. He, or she, was of Afro-Caribbean descent. The tone of the skin fragments which remained hanging from the leg was a giveaway. Some of the skeleton looked mummified.

"Carrion beetles here," said Shona. "Should help Mary to establish a timeline for death and burial. Iain, get one into the correct specimen pot and seal it tight."

"I'm impressed with the level of your knowledge, Ma'am," said Jason.

"It wouldn't hurt you to learn a thing or two." Her attention moved back to the limb.

"It's been there a lot longer than the other limbs," said Shona. "Difficult to tell if it's connected or not." She stopped and then shouted back to the team, "Who found him?"

"I'll go and ask Sergeant Muir," said Nina.

Sergeant Muir was the Police Official Licensed Search Advisor or POLSA for short. He secured the scene and dealt with all the comings and goings. Nothing happened without his say so. Shona might treat every crime scene like it belonged to her, but she was only second in the pecking order. Thankfully. Sergeant Muir liked her and let her run things to a certain extent.

Shona stood up and walked down the hill. There

were people everywhere, all of whom had a job to do and a role to play. There weren't many gawkers today. Probably due to the filthy weather thought Shona. It was difficult to tell who they were given the fog, but there was no mistaking one particular voice.

"I leave you to your own devices for a minute and the dead bodies pile up."

Shona swivelled, her face lit up by a dazzling smile. "Douglas."

Romance between Douglas and Shona usually meant a third wheel in the shape of a corpse. Shona wouldn't turn down the chance to see him, dead body or not.

"There's not much of a pile as there's only been a couple. This one is only an leg at the moment."

"So now you're turning your job into a human jigsaw puzzle?" The smile in his eyes turned Shona's legs to jelly.

She left him to climb up the hill towards the corpse, turned to Nina and said, "Where's our witness?"

Nina pointed her in the direction of an Indian woman who had a huge collie dog sitting at her feet. It looked as miserable as its owner.

As she walked up the dog gave a low growl. Tensed muscles indicated it was preparing to pounce. The owner stroked its head and it calmed down. Just as well thought Shona. The last thing I need is more shenanigans with dogs.

The woman's name was Abhijita Dhawan. "Call me Abi," she said with a tremor in her voice.

"DI Shona McKenzie." Shona put out her hand and the woman shook it with a trembling hand.

"Let's go into the café. They've opened it up for us and we can have a hot drink while we speak."

They trooped into the café and sat down with a

strong coffee and a camomile tea. The smell of the perfumed tea made Shona's stomach churn. She swallowed hard and let the woman sip in silence for a few seconds. As she drank the fragrant brew she stopped tembling.

"Could you tell me a bit more about what you found?"

"I was taking Raj for a walk. He was off the lead and I found him digging. I didn't want him to get too dirty so I pulled him away." She stopped.

Shona allowed her a few seconds to collect herself.

"Then?" Shona encouraged.

"Then I saw the l...l...leg." She started crying.

Shona handed her a tissue. "It must have been very difficult for you. No wonder you're upset."

The trumpet sound of an elephant reverberated around the room as Abi blew her nose. But the crying stopped. It was replaced by sniffing.

"Did you see anyone else around?"

"I think I saw a shadow disappearing into the mist. It could have been my imagination though. I was freaked out."

"I'm sure you were. Finding a human leg is enough to freak anyone out." Except me of course, thought Shona. If it's freakish it's on my docket.

She continued, "Do you walk your dog here often?"

"Most days. I live in Bingham Terrace. It's close so I don't have far to come."

"Have you ever seen anything out of the ordinary?"

"Not really. Even prossies are ordinary in here. I saw a couple of guys who could have been their pimps."

"I had heard. Can you describe them?"

"I might be able to."

She called over Roy and asked him to take Abi

down to the station. "Ask the profiler to work with her to get a photo together."

"That profiler's useless. The suspects are more likely to look like Shrek."

Shona thought longingly of the old profiler, Alexander Alexander or double Eckie as he was fondly known. He could draw pictures so good you could swear you were looking in a mirror. He was about eighty years old but no one had the heart to retire him. Ill health took the choice out of his hands and double Eckie was now staying with his daughter in Peebles.

"He's getting better. Give him a chance. Anyway that top of the range computer programme of his should help. You're a computer whizz. Surely you must be able to help."

By this point Abi was looking at her watch so Shona told Roy to hurry himself up. "She'll be too old to remember what they looked like by the time you get back to the station."

Two hours and a dog search later Shona was still crouched on the side of a hill. Once Mary had arrived more of the remains had been uncovered. This wasn't a single limb, but a whole skeleton. According to Mary it belonged to a male. She said she'd get the remains back to the mortuary once they'd had time to examine them in situ.

"Has the search thrown up anything else?" Shona asked Abigail who was standing nearby.

"I don't think this one's been out partying recently. Any evidence will be long gone."

"That's where you're wrong Watson. You'd be amazed at what can be seen when you look under the layers."

"Well unless it's going tae give us the name of the killer, could we go back to the station. I'm sodden through and cold as a newly caught kipper." Peter was practicing his usual sport of moaning. Shona reckoned he must be ready for the Olympics now.

Shona released them and made her escape. Fog wasn't the warmest of blankets. There were only so many times you could nip off for a scalding coffee at the site of a newly uncovered body.

10

Someone had turned the furnace up in the station. The heat hit them like a ten-ton truck. Steam rose off their clothes as they walked back to the office. Roy looked up from his computer.

"Where's Abi?" asked Shona.

"Still with Neill."

"For all that time. The poor woman must be losing the will to live."

"She looked happy as a clam when I left them to it. It seems they went to school together."

"We're not paying Neill to reminisce, we're paying him to produce profiles." She threw her coat on a nearby chair and stomped off. She managed to rein her temper in for Abi's sake. The woman had had enough traumas for one day.

"How is the profile coming along?"

Neill uncrossed his lanky legs, bent over the computer and swivelled the screen. "We're just done." He pushed his glasses up his nose with long fingers.

Two faces stared out of the screen. Shona took one look and was convinced they were guilty. Sullen faces and frowns the size of Scotland. They could be related. The only difference was the hair. One muddy blonde and the other grey and long. They looked the type to be going around murdering people. Shona had a sudden urge to murder them.

"Is that Jimmy McTaggart?"

"Who?" asked Neill.

Shona sighed. She'd give her right arm to have double Eckie back. He knew everyone and everything. "Never mind. Can I get a few print outs of that and can you email it to me?" She turned to Abi. "You've been very helpful. I'll get someone to take you home."

Once they were in the briefing room Peter handed her a roll with a couple of sausages on it. "Get that down you. It'll warm you up."

"Warm me up. It's like the Sahara desert in here."

"Ma'am. Please. Do me a favour and don't complain. They'll turn it down to zero." A panicked look had appeared on Jason's face.

"You wee sook. Can you not cope with a bit of cold? I thought you were mummy's wee soldier. Do they not do cold in the Army?" said Roy.

"I went to Afgahnistan. It was 150 degrees in the shade there."

"When you pair are finished squabbling you might want to join us on this case." Shona had scarfed down the roll and was ready for action.

With a slight movement and one click of a computer mouse two identikits appeared in huge glorious technicolour on the screen.

"Is that Jimmy McTaggart?" asked Nina.

"Cannae be. He's moved over to Glasgow to roll with the big boys," answered Peter.

"So whose that?" asked Shona. "His doppelganger?"

"It's probably his wee brother, Moose," said Peter.

"Moose? We're nowhere near Canada. Wherever did he get that nickname from?"

"No, not moose as in Elk. Moose, the Scottish for mouse. He was a timerous wee thing so his family gave him the nickname and it stuck."

"He doesn't look particularly timid now. In fact he makes me feel I wouldn't want to meet him in any alley, dark or otherwise."

"Your right. If you think Jimmy's a bampot he's like a lassie compared to Moose. There's a rumour that even the Alexeyev's won't take him on."

"I find that difficult to believe. He probably started the rumour himself."

"Who's the other bloke?" asked Jason.

"That's Eug MacBeatha, Moose's henchman," said Roy.

"I'm not even going to attempt to say that," said Shona.

"It's short for Eugene."

"Who, in Dundee, would saddle their child with a name like Eugene?"

"Why do you think it's shortened?" said Peter. "That's probably where he practiced his future career as a thug. Fighting off the school bullies."

Shona rolled her eyes. "Fetch the pair of them in."

All the men stood whilst the women remained seated. Sexism did not come into it when considering the likes of Moose and Eug. They took the word misogyny and elevated it to a higher level. Shona was happy to bide her time and wait until she had Moose in an interview room. Then she'd put him in his place.

Jimmy's brother was bellowing like the North American elk itself when he was dragged into the police station. Shona was glad to see that Jason, the catastrophe waiting to happen, was with the much calmer Eug. In fact Eug looked like a half shut knife as the saying went.

"Is he okay? He doesn't look quite right to me."

"High as a kite, Ma'am. I've no clue what he's on but he's in psychedelic cloud cuckoo land."

"Put him in a cell and get a Doctor in. We can't interview him like that."

"Okay dokey." Jason was high on the fact he'd managed an arrest without injury to himself. This fact was noteworthy enough that it could be sent out via interdepartmental email.

Whilst Shona waited for Moose to be bundled into an interview room, she went to find Abigail and Nina.

"Nina, I need you to scour missing persons for any outstanding cases where the missing person is Afro-Caribbean. Abigail, update HOLMES and see if we can find anything to remotely link our cases."

"Can't Roy do that? He's the computer maestro."

"Stop arguing Abigail and do what you're told. Roy and his muscles are going to be gainfully employed helping me to interview Moose."

"Interview with Mr Andrew McTaggert. DI Shona McKenzie, DS peter Johnston and DC Roy McGregor present. Mr McTaggert we need to ask you a few questions."

"Fu—"

Shona slammed her fist on the desk, got up and moved her face close to Moose's. "If even one swear word trips off that tongue of yours I'll cut it off," she said in a voice low enough it couldn't be heard by the recording."

She sat back in her chair. "So are we clear? I requested you not swear during this interview." Her voice was louder.

"You threatened me. I'll no hae a woman threaten me."

"I did no such thing. I merely politely asked you to stop swearing."

"I want my lawyer."

"I'm sure you do. It doesn't happen to be Margaret McCluskey or Angus Runcie by any chance?"

McCluskey and Runcie were brother and sister and the bane of Shona's life. Every low life in the City had one of them as their lawyer. Consequently, every time Shona turned round they were in the station.

Shona was astonished when the lawyer appeared. It was neither Angus nor Margaret. This was a lawyerly specimen Shona had never seen before. Tall, and ginger haired, his eyes exuded charisma. He held out his hand for Shona to shake.

"Henry St John-Smith." His voice was pure cut crystal. That alone indicated he came from money, and was English. How he ended up in Dundee was anyone's guess.

"DI Shona McKenzie. I'm the chief Investigating Officer."

Henry's handshake was no-nonsense firm.

Having taken one look, both Abigail and Nina were vying to be in the interview.

"Tough luck girlies. Peter and Roy have the privilege. Bampots need muscles and neither of you fit the bill."

"Aww, Ma'am. How come you get all the good jobs?" said Nina.

"Because I'm the boss. Anyway, won't your latest squeeze be upset that you're lusting after other men?"

"I'm between men at the moment."

For the second time that day Shona was astonished. "You? Between men? I never thought I'd hear that."

She dragged Peter and Roy in the direction of an interview room.

"Now you've got a lawyer, Moose, I hope you're going to be a bit more cooperative."

"I'm no' doing anything you say. Women should be in the hoose, cleaning."

"The women in your life might be happy to clean the house. I, on the other hand hold the most senior position around here. I'm sure I can find a reason to lock you up. You might want to think about that."

Henry's voice shifted from charismatic to full on lawyer. "Please do not threaten my client."

"I am not threatening him, I am explaining that all actions have consequences. Especially in my nick."

Their stares held until they broke them simultaneously. This was going to be some battle of wills thought Shona.

It would appear that you spend a lot of time in Baxter Park, Moose. Is that the case?"

"It's a public park. I'm entitled to be there."

"Don't get funny with me. I expect a proper answer."

"I gave you one. What more do you want."

Shona took a deep breath and turned to Henry. "Instruct your client to answer my question. If he doesn't, I swear I will find something to charge him with. I'm sure he's thigh deep in something illegal."

"Answer the DI's question Mr McTaggart. You

have nothing to hide."

"I was walking the dog."

"According to my witness the only creature, human or canine, that was with you, was Eug. He might be a bit on the simple side but he is definitely not a dog. Unless he transforms into a werewolf."

Moose leaned forward, placing his heavily tattooed forearms on the table. "Dinnae call my best pal that or I'll cut you. I'm warning you."

"Even someone as thick as you should know that it's not a good idea to issue threats in a police station. What were you doing in the park?"

"We were out for a wee walk."

"In a pea souper? Come on Moose. You can do better than that. I think you were out seeing your girls."

"Prove it."

"Funnily enough I'm not interested in that. I'm more interested in the provenance of a corpse we found there."

"What are you talking about?"

"I'll make it simple. Do you know where the dead body came from?"

"What dead body? I don't know anything about a dead body. What the fu..." The rest of his words were drowned out by the sound of a chair crashing to the ground. Peter and Roy leapt into action and wrestled him back down.

"Sit down Mr McTaggart." Shona's tone left no room for an opposite point of view. "Have you seen anything suspicious going on in that park during your nocturnal strolls?"

Moose's furrowed brows told Shona he couldn't quite cope with the big words. She tried again. "Have you seen anything strange in the park?"

"No. No way. No dead bodies."

"I'll need to interview your girls as well."

Moose opened his mouth.

"Don't even try to argue or I'll be arresting you for pimping. Give my Sergeants their names."

"You cannae charge me for being a pimp."

"You're absolutely right Moose. However, I can charge you for procuration of a woman to become a prostitute, exploitation of prostitution, and living on earnings of prostitution. Is that clear enough for you?" Shona hoped this would focus his mind.

They kept Moose incarcerated for a few hours. It gave them time to bring in the girls without him interfering. The station looked like a brothel and you could have cut the cloying scent of perfume with a knife. They were still no further forward. Shona repeated, "So you're telling me you saw nothing," so many times, she was thinking of having it tattooed on her forehead. Even the living on the earnings of prostitution threat of arrest did nothing to loosen their tongues. Shona was inclined to think they were telling the truth. However, someone must have seen a dead body being buried. She had to content herself with the fact that Dundee was the biggest village in the world. A guilty conscience might propel someone in the direction of the station. She was ever the optimist despite any evidence to the contrary in her career so far. In the meantime she now had the identity of two or three corpses to work out.

Returning to her office Shona took off her leather jacket and hung it on the back of one of the chairs. It had cost her an arm and a leg. Italian leather, it was pretty much the only expensive item of clothing she owned. She caught the flash of an excited puppy just in time. Fagin was heading towards the sleeve. The jacket was millimetres from the jaws of doom when she yanked it away, folded it carefully and placed it on top of the filing cabinet.

"The sooner Jock comes to get you, the better. We can't afford to have you here for much longer."

The puppy yipped and tried to bite her hand. She picked him up and cuddled him close. "Sorry pup, but I've work to do." Tail wagging Fagin licked her face with a tongue that meant business. She put him down, dried her face with one hand and picked up the phone with the other.

Before Shona could make the call, Nina barged through the door of her office. It never seemed to occur to Nina that she could knock. The puppy, shocked, leapt up and hurtled towards Shona.

"I've a couple of names that might fit the description of our corpse," Nina shouted over the yipping puppy.

"I'm glad you've got a good reason for taking the door off the hinges."

Nina grinned and said, "It could be Gabriel LaShawn or Delores Wasaki. They're the only two that fit the bill and have gone missing in Scotland.'

"See if you can pin down the whereabouts of their next of kin. I'll find out of the body belonged to a man or a woman."

She tried once again with the phone call.

"Our body from Baxter Park. Was it male or female?" she asked when the call was answered.

"Definitely male."

"We think it might be a chap named Gabriel LaShawn. Could you get a DNA sample?"

"It's all yours."

"Any joy with DNA on the limbs yet?"

'Miracles I can do almost straight away, the impossible takes a wee bit longer."

"I was living in hope."

"I'm sure you were but you'll have to exercise your patience genes."

"I think I was born without those particular genes."

"I had noticed. I'll be in touch the minute I have anything. In the meantime I'm sure it wont be long before you have another body to keep you occupied and me snowed under."

Deciding it was knocking off time Shona dismissed the troops.

"Enjoy your moment of respite before the next onslaught."

"I'll enjoy mine. I'm off on a date," said Nina."

"A date? You said you were between men. How on earth have you managed to find someone to date in the couple of hours since we had that conversation?"

"I'm going out with Henry."

"Henry? The lawyer?"

"Yep, Mr Charismatic himself."

"You can't date a lawyer involved in the case."

"I pinky promise there will be no pillow talk."

Shona gave up on the conversation and, shaking her head, dragged an exhausted puppy home.

Shakespeare, Shona's cat, met them at the door. Fagin dashed at the cat, resulting in her batting the dog's nose with a gentle paw. She then threw Shona a look that quite clearly said, "If that animal isn't out of here soon, I'm applying for adoption." She turned around, tail held high, and stalked off. Unperturbed, the puppy lolloped along beside her.

"He'll be gone soon. Don't get your whiskers in a twist, Shakespeare."

Shakespeare's frantic meowing indicated she shut up her mouth and open up a can of something delectable. Shona fed the pair of them and phoned for a pizza for herself. After all this wandering about the countryside searching for body parts, she needed to relax. Unfortunately she couldn't relax with Douglas and his kids as Alice had chickenpox. She poured herself a glass of Talisker and waited for the meat feast pizza to arrive. By the time it did Shakespeare and Fagin were cuddled up together fast asleep. "You're an old softy really, Shakespeare." The cat opened one eye and her stare said tell anyone and you're going to be served up for tomorrow's dinner. Shona picked up the remote for the television and curled up on the sofa. She switched on something requiring no brain power to watch.

11

He walked the streets at night his thoughts occupied with death. He was a young man who was sleepless and wandering aimlessly. This was the image he wanted to portray and did so effortlessly. Yet his mind was not aimless. The darkness allowed him to explore the evil that lurked on the underside of every city. How would one find victims? Who would make the best victims? Where would one meet them? These were the things he needed to know. The night was his to consider such issues.

The homeless perhaps? Vulnerable and no one caring for, or about, them. These would be ripe for the picking. They were dismissed, however, as being too difficult to transport without notice. He had to keep in mind that he would not be caught.

What about prostitutes? They would come with him willingly and it would be effortless to kill them. The middle of the sex act would be perfect. He filed this away in his brain as a definite possibility.

Children or teenagers would be easy to snatch and kill. Get to know them and lure them away. Their necks would snap with just one twist. But the police move quickly in such cases. This increased the chance of getting caught.

Even he couldn't go down the route of those with

special needs. Vulnerable they may be but he couldn't do that. Everyone has their own line that they will not cross no matter how bad the situation. This was his.

Each street, each step, brought fresh ideas. These were dismissed or filed for later use. These nocturnal walks fuelled his plan. They brought it ever closer to completion. This was his time. No one to intrude or chase his thoughts away.

12

A ringing doorbell wakened Shona from a nightmare. She was being suffocated by a trumpeting elephant firmly sitting on her chest. The minute she opened an eye the reason became apparent. Both Shakespeare and Fagin were lying on top of her and snoring fit to wake the dead. She struggled out from under them and hurtled towards the door. Its frantic ringing added to the cacophony of meowing and yelping in her flat.

"I'm coming. Take your finger of the blasted bell," she screamed to no avail.

She yanked the door open. It was Roy, kitted out in his usual designer elegance, and looking as bright as a Sergeant Major's buttons. She, in mismatched pyjamas and wild hair, felt like something out of Mary Shelley's Frankenstein.

"For heaven's sake Roy. This had better be good given it's 0437 and I've had about ten minutes sleep."

"We've another body part to investigate. You weren't answering your phone."

"It's charging in the lounge. What's up with the landline?"

"Deader than our corpses. Flooding in the exchange apparently."

"You're far too cheerful." She pointed him in the direction of the kitchen. "Make us coffee and toast. I'm sure the body part will wait another half an hour."

In her bedroom she threw on some chinos and a shirt, slapped a facecloth around various bits of her anatomy, and dragged a brush through her hair. Joining Roy in the kitchen she asked, "What particular body part is it."

"Another leg."

"I feel like I'm in some surreal universe playing a mixture of treasure hunting and human jigsaw."

"You're a genius, Ma'am. That's exactly what we're doing. Apart from the alternate universe bit."

"If I was that much of a genius I'd have solved this by now. We wouldn't be chasing around Scotland in the middle of the night. Where are we going by the way?"

"Westmuir Castle," said Roy as they hurried out the door ahead of their half hour schedule.

"Someone had the temerity to bury a body inside a stately home?"

"Maybe it's been there since the castle was built? They were always fighting in those days."

"It's chosen a funny time to reappear if that's the case."

They left Roy's car and Shona did a good impersonation of a rally driver in hers. They arrived at Westmuir in 13 minutes.

"Respect, Ma'am. You're a cracking driver," said Roy. He was grinning ear to ear.

"You've more stamina than soldier boy. He turns into a snivelling wee baby if I go over forty." She strode in the direction of the crime scene with Roy scurrying to catch up.

They weren't quite inside the castle gates. The POLSA had the road blocked off and wasn't letting a soul past the crime scene tape which went from pillar to strong stone pillar of the imposing entrance to the grounds. Huge iron gates, adorned with the family crest stood open beyond the tape. The branches of ancient trees hung low over the wall due to the weight of water from the torrential rain. Bulbous drops from the sky, mixed with a torrent of those from the trees, provided an invigorating shower. Convenient for anyone who'd missed their morning ablutions in their haste to attend the crime scene.

Shona flashed her ID to the young PC on the gate. He looked a bit nervous. This was probably because Shona had a go at him a couple of times on previous cases for allowing onlookers into the crime scene. No one wanted to get on the wrong side of Shona more than once. She then ducked under the tape, followed by Roy and Peter. It was immediately apparent where the crime scene was as they could see a foot sticking up from the sodden ground. There were also a couple of burly coppers shooing off what looked to be pigs. If Shona's guess was right they were wild pigs.

"Why are you lot running around my crime scene? Get those animals and your size fourteens out of here now."

"That's what we're trying to do."

"Who owns the blasted pigs?"

"The farmer over there. The one with the dog. They managed to break out in the night and he was looking for them. He saw the leg and called it in."

The elderly farmer, all seven foot of him, was calmly leaning against a tree, looking at the situation, with a smirk on his face.

"What are you laughing at? Get those pigs out of here and give a statement to my officer." She looked behind her and shouted. "Sergeant Chakrabarti get in here and interview Mr..." She looked over at the man.

"Duncan."

"Is that your first or second name?"

"Second. I'm Fergus Duncan."

He, and the dog, managed to round up the pigs, and Nina bore them all off through the gates. The crime scene was a churned up morass of leaves and mud, with a foot kicking up towards the sky. By this time the remainder of the team had joined them.

"Why is this case pigging well awash with animals?" said Shona.

Sniggers were stopped by Shona's fierce glance.

"You have to admit that was really funny, Ma'am," said Abigail.

"I wasn't trying to be funny. It's 5 a.m. and I've got the crime scene from hell. All you lot can do is laugh. Even without a crystal ball I can see a stint in traffic in your futures."

With much biting of lips and a somewhat eclectic mix of guttural sounds, the others managed to stop giggling.

It was obvious the leg wasn't historic. In fact Shona would bet her pay packet on it not having been there very long. It looked fairly fresh if somewhat muddy. Shona heard a voice behind her. One which made her weak at the knees and start to drool.

"What have you managed to do to that crime scene? It's spectacular even for you?"

Douglas handed her a large coffee cup filled with the scalding brew. She gratefully accepted it and took a restorative sip before saying, "Douglas. I thought Alice was ill? How come you've made it here?"

"I knew I had an early start this morning so my mum's over at my house. I didn't think it would be this early though." He stopped to appraise the crime scene. "Has someone been mudwrestling in there."

"You don't want to know. Suffice to say it involved pigs and policemen."

"Pigs and policemen? Are you sure this isn't a P.G. Wodehouse sketch."

"You'd think so. If I see another animal in this case I think I'll scream."

"The case. Where are you with it?"

"All over the countryside is where we are. Body

parts strewn in every shire and not a clue to be found."

"I'm sure you'll find some soon. How's Mary taking it all?"

"Like the trooper she is. She likes a puzzle."

"I'll have to go. Keep me updated with what's going on. Try to keep away from pigs."

"If a miracle should happen and we turn up a clue, you'll be the first to know."

Douglas sauntered in the direction of his car leaving Shona to the leg, the bottom of which was demonstrating a defiant pose as it stretched up for the heavens.

"It looks like a cricket stump."

"Roy, don't be so irreverent. This is someone's severed limb we're talking about."

"He's right though, Ma'am. It does kind o' remind you of cricket."

"I can't believe I'm hearing this. First football, and now cricket, all you lot ever talk about is sport."

"I quite like cricket," said Abigail.

"Who do you foll—" Jason is cut off in mid flow by an irate Shona.

"Stop with the cricket and start with the investigating. This is a crime scene not a school sports field. Where are Iain and the camera?"

They all looked round but he was nowhere to be seen. Shona whipped out her iPhone and dialled his number.

"Sorry, Ma'am. Had to get my next door neighbour to jump start the car. I'll be about ten minutes."

Shona shooed them all away from the spot and went to the gate to wait for Iain. He screeched to a halt, launched himself from the car, leaving his car door open in the process. He hurried over to her putting the lens on his camera as he went. Shona led him to the crime scene and he stopped short.

"What am I meant to photograph? Apart from the leg I mean. What's happened here?"

"Wild pigs is what happened." As Iain opened his mouth she said, "Don't even ask."

Iain got snapping from the periphery and Shona cast an eagle eye over the crime scene.

"Abigail and Jason, come with me." She indicated a tent, which had been set up for the donning of coveralls and overshoes.

"After the dancing pigs and overweight plods I don't know why we're bothering," said Jason.

"You're bothering because I said so. I'm sure if you use what's between your ears you'll figure out that we need to preserve any evidence that's left."

Silence reigned as they methodically searched the area, each taking their own segment. The tension as they tried to preserve the scene, could almost be sliced with a butter knife.

"There's some string here, Ma'am." Jason called over to her.

"Iain, crime scene bag and take it to the POLSA. Gently round the area."

Iain obliged, and the search continued until Mary turned up to claim the area.

"I'll take that foot off your hands, Shona."

"That sentence makes no sense but I know what you mean. Let me know when you're back at work. I need to come and see you."

"I'm all yours. I've got some information for you. Let's get this limb squared away first."

"You lot widen the search. Arrange to interview everyone up at the castle as well. I'm off back to the station to scour HOLMES."

She got as far as the gate when she bumped into a couple of reporters. Adanna Okifor, a tall black reporter, had turned up with her sidekick photographer. They worked for the *Dundee Courier*. Shona hated reporters with a vengeance, with good reason it turned out. However, Adanna was slightly more palatable than her associates. She genuinely seemed keen to work alongside Shona rather than make her life more difficult. That didn't mean that Shona trusted her yet.

"What do you want? I would have thought you'd be in your bed, not out here bothering me."

Adanna, who was used to Shona, took it in her usual implacable style. "I heard you were investigating a number of limbs that people have been digging up."

"How did you hear that? We've not released it yet."

"The whole of Dundee's talking about them. I didn't have to go far."

"It's the middle of the night. Dundee isn't talking about anyone. Everyone's asleep."

"Fergus Duncan is pals with my granddad. He gave him a ring and said I might be interested."

"If I get my hands on Fergus I'm throwing him under the hooves of a whole herd of wild pigs."

Adanna, showing not one jot or tittle of remorse, just laughed.

"I'll be holding a press conference later. Come to that." Shona turned to walk away then hesitated. Turning back she said, "Do not step past that gate. If any pictures of my crime scene appear in *The Courier* I will lock both of you up for the remainder of this case.

She could hear Adanna's trumpeting laugh as she walked away. Nothing could keep that woman down she thought.

On the way back to the shackles of her desk she managed to nip into Costa's and get a double shot espresso to assist her eyes in staying open. Then she popped into the bakers for half a dozen boxes of cream cakes. Nobody could cope with an early morning without a few million calories inside them. Fagin, as exhausted as Shona, curled up on his bed, the minute they got back to the office. He promptly fell asleep.

"Thanks for your support, Mutt."

The puppy didn't twitch a muscle. At least the station was safe from his capers for a while thought Shona. She fired up her top of the range Mac Computer and went to brew a large pot of strong Brazilian Arabica. She'd long ago decided that it was better to bring your own than drink the muck the station served as coffee. She was soon on HOLMES searching for any cases linked to body parts. The only thing HOLMES threw up was in Nottingham. She picked up the phone to dial the local coppers. She was stunned at the news they gave her.

"Someone at the hospital who was supposed to incinerate amputated limbs, was spreading them around the countryside. She thought it would be fun to see if the police could solve it."

"What? I take it she's now serving time in the nearest prison?"

"Tucked up as tight as in Broadmoor. Loopy as they come."

"It's not her then. Could be a copycat. Thanks."

By the time she'd finished the chief had arrived. She brought him up to date and added, "I've made an appointment to see the chief Executive at Ninewells Hospital. She's free in an hour so I'm heading off."

"Can't you use one of those state of the art phones you've all been issued with?"

"I could Sir, but I may need to investigate further. I've asked Sgt Johnson to meet me there."

She was speaking to the chief's bald head as per usual. She wondered if she could batter him about the bald head with said phone. The judge knew the chief, or Thomas as he probably called him. She might just get away with it as being justified on grounds of sanity. Keeping her sanity that is.

She abandoned her car on some double yellow lines at the entrance to the hospital. Her official police warning should see her through. The buses and taxi's would be able to get past and no one else was allowed up that bit of the road. She met Peter outside WH Smith where he was perusing a copy of *The Courier*.

"Anything in there about our case?" asked Shona.

"Nothing. They're too busy worrying about flooding."

Shona perked right up. "Has *The Courier* building been flooded?"

"No. They're talking about the flooding everywhere else."

"Oh well. I can but hope."

"What have you got against the press anyway?"

"You need to ask that? You must have a short memory. Come on, we need to stop champing our gums and get a move on."

The chief executive was both charming and helpful.

"I am one hundred per cent certain that the body parts did not originate here, but you are more than welcome to investigate. My secretary will help you in any way you want."

The secretary called in the staff who would deal with this and they brought the relevant paperwork with them. However, they needed a warrant to check it against patient records. Sherriff Struthers was more than happy to provide the necessary warrant and blue lighted it across to the hospital. The PC who hurtled through the doors with it was, Brian Gevers.

"Brian. Good to see you. Thanks for getting it here so quickly."

"I had a blast dodging the traffic on a blue light. Great fun."

"Boys and their toys."

"Ma'am, you've got a real cheek. You drive like that without blue lights," said Peter.

"Moving swiftly on." She snatched the warrant from Brian and handed it to the waiting technicians. It wasn't long before they surmised that all amputated limbs for the last several years were correctly accounted for.

"A dead end then."

"You're a laugh a minute, Ma'am."

"If that's the best I can do then I won't give up the day job. I'm going to go see Mary at the mortuary before I come back to the office. I'll see you there."

"I'll probably be in the canteen. I'm Hank Marvin."

"You might be starving, but you've still got to heed the wife's instructions to watch what you eat."

"That'll be right. I'll be tucking into a full Scottish breakfast with all the extras I can pile on the plate."

Shona just shook her head and hurried towards her car.

13

He bought a hard backed notebook and a black pen. The notebook was unremarkable. Nothing to distinguish it. Not so the contents. This was his research on the different types of people he could kill. Each page was headed and then beneath, two columns were neatly drawn - for and against. He would add to this as his research grew and matured. As his thoughts clarified. He did not have all the answers yet. One day this would change.

No one paid him any heed at home. He had an amiable relationship with his parents. They let him come and go as long as his school marks were maintained. He made sure they were. This meant that no one noticed what he was doing or the lists he compiled. An only child he was no trouble. Little did his parents know what kind of son they were raising. What his career aspirations were. They would never know. He would see to that.

Day by day, week by week, year by year, the chilling dossier grew. One more step closer.

14

The station now had a brand new mortuary, state of the art, and cutting edge in more ways than one. The funds had been raised by a number of crime writers and it was named after one of the finest of them - The Val McDermid Mortuary. A rather grisly way to be immortalised thought Shona. However, she was prepared to give in to higher powers on the matter. Mary had made herself at home and her office looked as cheery and welcoming as always. The bright rugs and vivid paintings were a direct contrast to the clinical professionalism of the stainless steel mortuary. Shona didn't have time to park her bottom in a seat before Mary dragged her into the mortuary.

"You'll want to see this."

The body from Baxter Park was lying on one of the tables. Mary rolled him over and there was a piece of rusty metal sticking from his back.

"What's that? It doesn't look like a bullet."

"A crossbow bolt."

"I'd heard the good folks of Dundee like to shoot each other with those but that's the first I've come across it."

"That's because they're all rubbish at it. They're more likely to be in Casualty getting wounds stitched, than lying on my tables. Whoever did this knew exactly what they were doing and they meant business. They've used a 20 inch four hundred grain crossbow bolt. To get it that accurate I'd say they needed a trajectory of —"

"Mary, speak human. I don't speak crossbow."

"This is a professional hit. Whatever, our lad did, he pissed off some of the big boys."

"Great. Just what I need when I'm trying to solve the mystery of the scattered limbs. Two cases at once."

"The Mystery of the Scattered Limbs. It sounds a bit like an Enid Blyton book."

"I'm beginning to feel like I'm in an Enid Blyton book, with Fagin standing in for Timmy the dog."

"Who's Fagin?"

Shona gave her the lowdown on the pup.

"Och, that's so nice, Shona. Jock will love him."

"That's if Jock ever comes to claim him. We haven't seen hide nor hair of him."

"After his recent business I'm sure he won't have gone far."

Returning to Bell Street, Shona found Fagin chewing on a ham sandwich. Where it had come from was anyone's guess.

"Listen here Fagin. If you want to stay then you need to stop thieving."

"Talking tae yourself are you, Ma'am?" Peter, had strolled into the room. "I've got Jock in one of the interview rooms like you asked. He's scoffing a couple of cakes and drinking tea as we speak."

"Thank goodness for that. Let's go and introduce this little bundle of trouble to his new master."

The puppy took one look at Jock, lolloped over and begged to be petted. Jock obliged. "You're a fine wee laddie." He looked up. "When did you get a dog, Shona? Maggie would have loved him."

"He's not mine Jock. He's yours." She hesitated. "If you want him?" Nobody had thought to ask Jock if he wanted another dog.

Jocks eyes filled with tears. He couldn't talk.

"Jock, you don't have to take him. We'll sort something out."

"I want to take him. He's that wee though I'm worried about him being on the street."

"We've arranged accommodation for you both. He comes with everything he needs. You've got to stay inside until he's bigger."

Tears were rolling down Jock's cheeks. "I will. You're a kind lassie. Has he got a name?"

"We've been calling him Fagin. He's a right little tea leaf."

At the sound of his name the dog wagged his tail.

"Aye. I like that name. Hello Fagin."

It was a match made in heaven. Shona had a feeling that all would be well in Jock and Fagin's world.

Shona called a copper to take man and dog to their lodgings. Fagin went off happily enough, tail wagging.

Shona felt a little bereft but got over it by calling the team to the briefing room. She outlined what had happened in the mortuary and the momentous discovery of the crossbow bolt.

"So it looks like a professional hit. Peter, in your experience is there anyone we could put the collar on for this?"

"The only professionals we have round here are the Alexeyevs. The rest of them swagger around like they're the business but they're just a bunch of low life scum," replied Peter.

"I always thought Gregor and Stephan were low life scum," said Abigail.

"You know what I mean. Dinnae split hairs."

"You're right. The Alexyevs are the real deal. The others are just like wee boys playing gangsters. Go fetch the twins," said Shona.

No one moved.

"Sorry, am I not speaking English clearly enough for you. I could swear I just gave an order."

"The twins won't come easily, Ma'am. Can we sign out guns," said Jason.

"You're obsessed with guns. You're not in the Army now you know. You've got a point though. I'll sign for Abigail, Jason, Iain and Roy to take guns out. You can fetch them."

"The chief will no' be happy, Ma'am."

"By the time I tell him you'll be long gone. It'll be too late then."

"What are you lot going to be doing while we're playing Russian roulette," asked Roy.

"Don't be so dramatic, Roy. We're going to fetch Moose. There's a whisper in the bazaars that he's in the employ of our merry band of Russian brothers."

"God help us all," said Peter, and he crossed himself. That just about summed it up perfectly.

Neither the Alexeyevs nor Moose were keen to help the police with their enquiries. Subsequently, there were a couple of minor injuries. Funnily enough Jason was amongst them. Either Gregor or Stephan, they were never sure which was which, had stamped on his foot. It was a bit swollen and bruised but he insisted he was fine. Nina had a black eye and they were about to charge Moose with Assault on a Police Officer. They'd have to work out who was who, and which of them actually injured Jason before they could charge them with anything. Surely other Inspectors don't have all these problems thought Shona.

"I'm thinking of applying for a transfer to a more peaceful force. The Highlands and Islands can't have all these goings on surely?"

"Och, Ma'am, you'd no sooner get there than dead bodies would start piling up," said Peter.

Shona sighed. "You're right. They seem to follow me around. Come on, you can help me interview one of the twins."

In order to establish which of the twins they were interviewing they had to check his fingerprint. Different experiences in the womb mean that even identical twins can be differentiated by their paw prints.

While they were waiting for the results the Alexeyev boys rang their lawyers. Gregor was represented by Angus Runcie, and Stephan by the Battleship McCluskey. Shona couldn't believe she had the Russians, Moose and two dodgy lawyers all at once. She was thinking all she needed now was Jimmy McTaggart to turn up and complete the unfortunate hand that fate had dealt her that day. The only thing that cheered her up was Roy handing her something he'd found on the Internet.

"Roy, I could kiss you."

"Anytime, Ma'am, but I don't want to get on the wrong side of the Procurator fiscal."

"Interview with Stephan Alexeyev blah, blah, blah." The initial proceedings over Shona continued. "Stephan, can you please tell me what you know about Crossbows?"

"You will call me Count Alexeyev."

"Since when have you gone by that moniker."

"I am Russian Royalty. You will treat me accordingly."

"You're Russian scum and I'll quite happily treat you that way."

The waiting Roy placed a firm hand on Stephan's shoulder to stop his rise from the chair.

"Sit down. The Inspector isn't finished with you yet."

"You can't talk to my client like that."

"Oh, belt up. I've had enough of you and your client already. Tell him to answer my question."

The battleship's chest seemed to get bigger. Shona was surprised to see this as she thought it was big enough already. Maybe Margaret McCluskey would explode and give them all something to celebrate. However, she just said, "Stephan, answer the question."

"I know nothing about crossbows."

Shona slammed a pile of papers on the desk and moved them over towards Stephan. "That's funny, because here all this says you've been involved with Crossbows since you were taking your mother's milk. For someone with no knowledge that's some rap sheet with the weapon."

"These are all lies. I was not charged with any of these."

"There seem to be an awful lot of alleged offences for someone who's innocent."

Stephan opened his mouth but McCluskey beat him to it. "My client is right. None of these alleged offences resulted in a charge."

Shona changed tack.

"Do you know a Mr Gabriel LaShawn?"

"I do not know this name." His piercing ice blue eyes dared her to say otherwise.

Shona passed a photo across the table and said, "You and your brother appear quite chummy with him here."

"I do not know who he is. Someone must have taken the picture with phone."

"So you're telling me you posed for a photo with someone you didn't know?"

"I was speaking to the man. Telling him I was not interested in any business deal. I did not know who he was."

At the moment Shona didn't have anything to prove otherwise. "I'm letting you go, but trust me I'm going to be looking into everything you do and how often you've been seen alongside Mr LaShawn."

The battleship McCluskey sailed off towing her client alongside. Shona repeated the interview with Gregor and Angus Runcie. Not only were the twins identical but so was the interview. They didn't have a thing to link the twins and the corpse except a photo.

The interview with Moose was slightly more enlightening. Moose was as thick as Scotts Porridge Oats, so couldn't hide anything if he tried. The charismatic Henry was accompanying him and Shona had banned Nina from the interview room.

"You get to whisper sweet nothings to your boyfriend over a crime scene. How come I'm being chucked out?"

"You're not being chucked out, you're being denied entry. Douglas and I both have to be at a crime scene."

"Well, I still think you're being a bit snotty."

"Don't talk to me like that. Around here I'm your boss and not your friend. Stop acting like a teenager and go and arrange a skype interview with Gabriel's next of kin. You can do it."

After the recording preliminaries were over Shona asked, "Moose, did you know a man named Gabriel LaShawn?"

"Me? Know a man wi' a pansy name like that? No way."

She passed the missing persons photograph across the table.

"That's no' Gabriel whatever you said his name was."

"How do you know?"

"Because that's Angel."

"Why was he called Angel?" Shona felt like knocking the stupid git into the middle of next week.

"I'm no' telling you."

Shona stood and loomed over Moose. "Answer my question. Now."

"I'm no' squealing to the pigs."

"If you don't answer my damn question you'll be squealing for real."

Henry decided it was time to butt in. "You can't threaten my client. He hasn't been arrested so you can't keep him here either."

"I'm going to arrest him in a minute for withholding evidence. If he wants to keep quiet then Gabriel—"

"I told you. That's Angel."

"—Angel was up to something dodgy. Now why was he called angel?"

"Because he's a pusher. Deals in Angel Dust." A penny must have dropped in his thick skull. "Why do you keep saying was. Is he dead?"

"We don't know. Do you think he could have been called Angel, because of his name?"

"What? That is his name."

Shona had a sudden urge to go and fetch a gun and shoot Moose. She'd be doing the world a favour.

"How did you know Angel?"

"Doing this and that. He was a worthless piece of Sh—"

"Mr McTaggart. That is quite enough. You will not use profanity in my station."

"You what?"

"Stop swearing."

"I'll speak any way I want. I'm not going to do what any woman tells me."

"This woman can lock you in a cell and throw the

key into the middle of the Tay estuary. You might want to remember that."

Moose snapped his mouth shut. Shona wanted to wipe the look of his sullen face.

"Do you know the Alexeyev's?"

"That pair o' pansies. Only to order them around."

"I'll tell them you said that. I'm sure they will be delighted."

Moose's leg started to beat a tattoo on the floor. He looked somewhat anxious. In fact he looked terrified.

"Calm down, Moose. Your secret's safe. Did the Alexeyev's and Angel know each other?"

"I think he worked for them. Dinnae tell them I said that."

"You're free to go Moose."

Moose bolted, Shona gathered up her papers and she and Peter walked back to the office. "How can anyone as stupid as Moose build up a reputation as a hard nut."

"It's because he's thick he's a bampot. Nothing scares him."

It turned out Gabriel's parents had moved back to Detroit. They were obviously so distraught about their missing son that they upped and left him to it. Nina had left a message saying she could skype them on her return. Nina had tried but they weren't available. She thought Shona would want to ring them herself if she could. Shona fired up Skype and broke the news that they may have found the missing Gabriel.

She was brewing some more coffee when the team piled in to the kitchen.

Roy piped up, "DI Shona McKenzie, saving the world one coffee at a time." He grabbed one of the last remaining cream cakes.

"It's better than saving the world one pie at a time."

"It's no' a pie it's a peh." Peter could always be relied upon to make sure Dundonian was spoken in the correct way.

"Whatever. Remember it's English round here. I haven't got time to be looking at a phrase book every five minutes."

"You should be able to speak and understand Scottish by now," said Nina. "You've been here forever."

Shona, was born in Dundee but not bred. Her father's job bore her off to Oxford when she was two. This meant she sometimes struggled with Scottish words. Although she had improved.

"The lot of you can shut up about my shortcomings in the form of Scottish vernacular. A brand new team is sounding good right about now."

"You love us really, Ma'am." Abigail had the last word on the subject. She was obviously feeling brave.

"I've been hearing rumours that Brian Gevers is engaged?"

"He is," said Iain. "To Fiona."

"How come I'm the last person to find out about these things? Have a whip round and get them a present and a card. Nina, you're good at these things. You're in charge."

Picking up a cream cake Shona took her spoils back to her office.

She picked up the phone and dialled Mary's number.

"Mary, have you—" She stopped dead at the sight that greeted her.

"I'll have to go, there's a lamb in my office." She hung up.

The door to her office had been pushed open and there was, indeed, a lamb standing in the doorway. It was bleating piteously, a sound which indicated he, or she, was missing his or her mother. What with dogs, pigs and now lambs she couldn't seem to move without tripping over an animal. She picked the lamb up and gently carried it to the office.

"Anyone know where this came from?"

"Soldier Boy found it wandering along the pavement so brought it in."

"No I never. You said we should bring it in."

"If you pair want to be alive at Christmas you'd better stop the squabbling."

The pair looked at each other and then her.

"Jason," she looked at Roy and continued, "and only Jason, where did this animal come from and who brought it here."

"Roy, and I, saw it wandering up Bell Street. We brought it in."

"It's a live animal, what made you think it was a good idea to bring it here?"

Roy said, "We thou—"

"I don't want to hear. The pair of you take it up to Camperdown Wildlife Centre and let them deal with it. I'll think of a suitable punishment in the meantime."

The pair left and Shona said, "I think I preferred it when that pair were fighting." Then she thought back to the time when she'd caught them beating the crap out of each other and changed her mind.

The other's couldn't answer they were laughing so hard.

"I don't think it's funny. How can we possibly have a lamb wandering around in here in October anyway? It's too late for lambs."

"Fall lambing, Ma'am. You don't get it much in the UK but it can be done," said Abigail.

"You lot know the weirdest things." With that she turned tail and marched back to her office.

She rang Mary, who said, "Did you just say there

was a lamb in your office?"

"I did." She explained the situation.

"Your cases are never dull. Puppies, lambs and pigs. Whatever next? I take it your ringing to find out about the DNA results?"

"I dread to think. Are the results in?"

"That they are, two limbs and two different women. Obviously we're still waiting for the results on this morning's offering."

"What? So it looks like someone is chopping up bodies and scattering the limbs to all corners of the earth."

"All corners of Scotland anyway."

"Are you able to tell what age they are."

"Roughly twenty eight to forty I'd say."

"Not again. Where do I even start investigating this?"

"Don't ask me. However, from the hairs on the limbs I'd say two were blonde and one auburn if that helps."

"It helps a lot. You've rocketed to the top of my Christmas card list." They said their goodbyes and Shona hung up.

She briefed the team and set them on a hunt for any missing women in the age range. "Do it five years younger and older. Just in case there's margin for error."

"Mary won't be wrong. In all my time working with her she's always got it right," said Peter.

"I agree. However, just in case this is the one time she hasn't got it right then we'll err on the safe side. If nothing else it'll keep you lot gainfully occupied."

A couple of hours later she was interrupted right in the middle of taking a bite of her cream cake, by Nina crashing through the door. This resulted in her smearing cream all over her face. As she grabbed a tissue to wipe her mouth she said, "Nina, you've got to get into the habit of knocking, or at least coming in more quietly."

"Sorry. We've finished. Narrowed it down to seven women."

"Okay. Grab the others I'll meet you in the briefing room."

"Where are the seven women from?"

"Five from Dundee, one from the Isle of Skye and one from Glasgow," said Nina.

"The only thing the Isle of Skye and Dundee have in common is Abigail," said Iain.

Abigail had joined them a couple of years back. She was from the Isle of Skye, her parents having settled there from Hong Kong.

"I'm sure that link isn't important. Abigail gets enough notoriety being part of this team," said Shona. "Abigail, do you know the missing woman," she glanced at her notes, "Henrietta Hardy?"

Jason wrote the name on the whiteboard alongside the pictures of the severed limbs.

"Nope. It's not a name I recognise. If there was anyone called Henrietta on Skye I'd know it. She must be a recent import."

"You get on to pinning down her next of kin. I'll leave you to talk to them, and get DNA. Nina, you're on Glasgow. The rest of us will cover Dundee."

Twenty minutes later Shona and Roy found themselves walking down Step Row, a steep cobbled street in the older end of town. The area hadn't changed much since the poet McGonagall had lived in nearby Paton Lane. Shona had learned that McGonagall, a beloved of Dundee, had actually been immortalised as the worst poet in the world. Shona agreed with that statement.

Not that she would ever say that to any Dundonian. She approached the front door of an enormous brown stone house and knocked. A middle-aged man opened it.

"Mr Peirs?"

"What do you want?"

They flashed their ID cards. "Detective Inspector McKenzie and my colleague, Detective constable McGregor. May we come in."

The man held the door open and said. "Aye."

Once they were seated in the vast living room he said, "We're pestered with cold callers here. Phone and door, there's never a minutes peace.."

"We need to speak to you about your wife."

"Have you found her? She's been missing for months."

"We're not sure, but we will need something like her hair brush or toothbrush."

"Is she dead? Have you found her body?" Tears spilled from his now vacant eyes.

"It's too early to say. Is there anything you can give us."

"I haven't got anything. I got rid of it all a few weeks ago. By then I knew she wasn't coming back."

Strange behaviour, thought Shona. You'd think he'd keep something.

"Any of her jewellery?"

"No. Nothing."

"Do you mind if we have a look around?"

"Why would you want to now? Go ahead anyway."

They had a quick but efficient look. Mr Peirs might have got rid of Anya's stuff but he wasn't a very good housekeeper. There was a long auburn hair behind the toilet bowl.

"What did your wife's hair look like?"

"Brown. She was growing it so a bit long."

"Like this?" Shona held up the evidence bag that

now contained the hair.

"Yeh. That's hers. What do you want it for?"

Shona hid her surprise. Surely there couldn't be anyone alive who couldn't work that one out.

"DNA. We will be in touch."

Shona sent all the DNA samples off to the lab the minute she returned to the station. They had managed to get something from all five girls in Dundee. Jason and Abigail assured her that it was all in hand at the other locations. They now had to play another waiting game. This was not something Shona was good at.

"Roy, I want you to look into the life of Bertram Peirs. See if there's anything in his past that might indicate he's killed now. I want to know everything about him, right down to whether he has hairs in his nostrils."

"You'll have a dossier as thick as one of Peter's sarnies."

"Peter's what?"

"Sandwiches."

Shona spent the remainder of the day looking up cases internationally where missing limbs had played a part. This was so fascinating it was gone six before she realised it.

She went to make sure the team were headed home and to find out from Roy what the score was with Bertram. The team were in the process of putting on coats and grabbing handbags. Roy was nowhere to be seen.

"Roy hasn't gone already has he?"

"Nah, he's just gone to get changed," said Nina.

Before she could ask what was going on, Roy came into the office, dressed in a magnificent cloak and a top hat.

"What on earth are you wearing?" asked Shona.

Moments later she regretted asking the question.

"I'm going to a fancy dress party." He whipped open the cloak and, underneath, was nothing more than a pair of scarlet coloured, silk boxer shorts.

Shona's brain, not usually short of a word, couldn't formulate one. After she managed to close her jaw she said, "What on earth are you going as?"

"Jack the Stripper." He grinned.

Everyone burst out laughing.

"Do you no' mean Jock the Stripper?" asked Peter.

By this point even Shona couldn't keep a straight face.

"Get out of here before the chief comes in to find out what's happening."

With a dramatic swirl, which left nothing to the imagination, Roy bolted out of the door.

"I swear that boy get's worse every day," said Shona.

"You've got to admit he's brightened everyone's day though," said Nina. "I haven't laughed so much in a long while."

On the way home Shona rang Douglas. It would appear that Alice was no longer in quarantine. He still couldn't go out and leave her, but they would all love Shona to come and visit. Shona turned the car in the direction of Domino's pizza. It would also appear that Douglas hadn't even thought about what they were having for tea. This ticked all the boxes. It would also make up for the fact that she was appearing without Fagin. The kids had grown very fond of the puppy.

Once the kids were in their jammies and tucked up in bed, the adults sank down on to the leather couch. After a couple of whiskies Shona was ready to open up and talk. Since her last case she'd been finding it difficult to go out on a case. Her stomach tightened and she felt physically sick at the thought. She had to force herself out. She couldn't focus and felt nervous all the time.

"I can't do this. They need to get someone who has at least one ounce of a clue. I give up." She took another slug of Talisker.

"Rubbish. Not only are you the best person for the job, you're the only person for the job," said Douglas.

"I very much doubt it."

"Shona I've had just about enough of this. Take a look at your track record and just get on with solving your case."

"That's easy for you to say. "

"This isn't the Shona I fell in love with. She was feisty, a fighter. Reach inside and find her again. Drag her out screaming if you have to."

"I..."

"I'm not interested." He grabbed the bottle of whisky. This stuff isn't helping."

"You can't tell me what to do."

"Yes I can. In the morning, get up early and go for a run. You need to start acting normally again and your old blood and guts gung ho attitude will come raging back. You'll see."

15

How did one kill someone? His research had moved on. He still hadn't perfected the art of disposing of a body but ideas were swirling around in his mind. He was allowing them to stay there. They would mix together until the perfect chemical combination of ideas sparked caused a eureka moment to explode in his brain.

Yet his mind was also consumed with the perfect way to kill. Books on poisons were devoured, as well as guns, bullets, strangling and many others that few people had heard of. He knew more about blow pipes than any other person living. The intricacies of the human body were like meat and drink to his developing mind. His parents encouraged him to study. A brilliant child, of brilliant free spirited parents he was pretty much left to read what he wanted. No one noticed the grizzly nature of his chosen literature. If they did then they didn't care enough to comment.

He read books and magazines about serial killers. He did this in the library without the books being signed out. Paper, and pen just another schoolboy working for exams. University was the same. No one was interested in what he was up to. He devoured each book and took careful notes. Later in his room he would cross reference and work out what might work and what might not.

Otherwise he was the life and soul of the party, one of

the boys. A rugby player, the teams for both school and university sought him out. He was improving his natural skill of hiding his true thoughts and feelings. Not just that but his true nature. His evil thoughts were pushed into an inner sanctum known only to him. This thrilled him more than anything else in this life ever could. He was master of his own destiny. Born to a greatness that he would one day fulfill.

16

The next morning, from somewhere deep inside Shona found a glimmer of her old self. She leapt out of bed and donned her running gear before she could change her mind. Douglas was right. The run was blowing away the cobwebs in a rather spectacular fashion. There was a strong wind blowing in from somewhere with arctic conditions. It whipped the North Sea into a frenzy and drove needle sharp drops of rain into her face. It felt invigorating and she could feel some of her va va vroom speeding back in time with her rhythm. Her legs moved faster as she ate up the miles along the sea front. Each thump of her foot brought her one step closer to being her old self - a strong willed officer with a steely determination to solve her cases. The run cleared her mind and gave her thinking space. Why were severed limbs from different suspects turning up in Scotland? Was it different cases which merely happened to have the same modus operandi. Highly unlikely, she thought. What could link them then? Difficult to say until they knew for certain exactly to whom they belonged.

She had arranged a press briefing for that morning. The chief was somewhat unimpressed, as he had arranged to go and play golf with the chief superintendent and some other bigwigs first thing. This came under the heading of a breakfast meeting. The golf was a team building exercise. Yeah right. The nearest she'd come to a team building exercise was a couple of hours running around in the mud doing an assault course. By the end of it the team weren't united but hated each other. Roy and

Jason had almost come to fisticuffs through acting like rutting stags. They were both trying to come first. They had to be put in separate offices for the rest of the week. Shona had managed to calm the chief down by telling him the press briefing would be at 11 am. He said he, and the chief super would be there. In honour of the occasion Shona had on a green, raw silk dress which showed off her lithe figure to perfection.

"What's with the frock, Ma'am? Have you got a modelling gig?" was Peter's response.

"Is the procurator fiscal on his way over?" asked Nina.

"No and no as you both fine well know so shut it. There's a press briefing later. The chief Super is coming as well so you'd better get this pigsty tidied up and look spick and span yourselves."

"Got it. We'll be great Mrs Mops," said Peter.

"I jolly well hope so. Also look busy. Roy, I need you to get those fingers moving over the keyboard and delve into the darkest depths of the Internet. We need as much up to date info as possible on the Alexeyevs and Moose. I think they're up to their unmentionables in dastardly deeds, and I intend to prove it."

"So you want to know what colour underwear they wear?"

"Pretty much."

"I'm on it." He scurried back to his computer.

"You're no' getting out of the cleaning that easy."

"Let him sort his own desk out Peter. Maureen's still about somewhere. Give her a holler and she'll help you."

"I might just do that. With the cleaner of the year on the case we'll be done in a jiffy."

At 11 o'clock precisely the suited and booted senior officers were standing in front of the gathered press.

Everyone had tipped up including STV and the BBC. Shona's cases were always big news in Scotland. The chief superintendent took the lead. This case was Scotland wide so it needed a bigwig as spokesperson. Shona didn't mind in the slightest that she was sidelined for this particular job. She hated giving press briefings.

"Police Scotland can today report that severed limbs have been found in three separate regions of Scotland. These have come to light over the past few days. We cannot say at present who the victims are but they are believed to be female. We have spoken to some families of missing women. We would like to assure the public at this time that the Police are doing everything in their power to catch the person, or persons, responsible. We are following a number of leads and several people are currently helping us with our enquiries. At this time we have no suspects. The police are appealing for information from anyone who may have seen anything out of place or any suspicious vehicles in the following areas - Inveraray, The Dundee Law, or Westmuir Castle. If any member of the public has information which could lead to an arrest in this case, then please contact the chief Investigation Officer, Detective Inspector McKenzie on 0300 572 8761."

Questions seemed to come from everywhere. As usual the Dundee reporters managed to get a question heard.

"Is this related to the case a few years back where young women were being killed?" asked Adanna.

"That is unlikely," said the chief superintendent.

"So you don't think it is the same killer."

"We are absolutely certain it is not," said Shona. Given the current whereabouts of that particular killer it was impossible she thought.

"Why are you so certain?"

"You're beginning to sound like a cracked record. Has anyone got any sensible questions?"

The chief superintendent stepped in. That will be all Ladies and Gentlemen.

The chief dragged Shona away.

"Shona, you shouldn't let them rattle you like that. I know they can be difficult but you must remain civil," said the chief superintendent.

"Yes, Sir. Sorry, Sir.

"I will talk to you later, Inspector," said the chief.

Shona knew she was for the high jump and made a mental note to stay clear of the chief for the foreseeable future. Maybe a year would be about long enough.

Whilst Shona had been annoying the bosses, Roy had been hard at work ferreting out information on the Alexeyevs. He hadn't come up with anything concrete on them, but did have some interesting information.

"It would seem that there are some new players in town. A bunch of Romanians headed up by Bogdan Petrescu. He's muscling in on the Alexeyev's territory."

"Interesting. Do you think Russian 1 and 2 have taken out one of Petrescu's boys to send a message?"

"You can bet you're a…. assets I do."

"Where will we find Petrescu?"

"That's the million-dollar question. We're not sure of his haunts as yet."

"Get the team in the briefing room. Let's see if anyone knows."

The team didn't have a clue. The nearest they got was Peter saying, "They're probably somewhere the Russians are not. Eliminate Gregor and Stephan's hangouts and it'll narrow things down."

"Good plan."

This still left a lot of places that they would have to search.

"Anyone got a tame informant in their back pocket?" asked Shona.

"We've been protecting Chick Anderson so he's been helping us out when we need it,' said Peter.

"Have we? How come I never knew about this?"

Peter opened his mouth but Shona said, "Never mind. Go and bring him in."

"He's no' that amenable."

"Bring him in anyway."

"Anyone else?"

"I've got a good relationship with Senga Rathbone. I'll have a word and see what she has to say for herself," said Abigail.

Peter was right. Chick wasn't happy to be back in Bell Street station. He was a pawnbroker who was as bent as a boomerang. Like the boomerang he kept coming back. He'd assisted in their enquiries a couple of years back and as a result was on the Alexeyevs hit list.

"How come you lot keep arresting me for nothing."

"We've not arrested you. We only want to ask you a few questions."

"That pair," he indicated Peter and Jason. "Put handcuffs on me."

"I assume you didn't want to come quietly?"

"Why the fu—"

Shona interrupted. "Now, now, Chick. You know the rules about swearing in my nick."

"How would I want to help you?"

"Because if you don't we'll feed you to the lions in the form of a pair of gangster Russians."

"What do yi want."

"Do you know anything about a man named, Gabriel LaShawn."

"Angel. He's a pusher. God knows what he's doing in Dundee. I think he's American."

"Was doing in Dundee. It appears he's now dead."

"What? Are you saying it was me? I never—"

"Save your breath to cool your porridge. I'm only asking if you knew him. Do you know anything about Bogdan Petrescu and his mob?"

"I can't inform on them. They're mad. Even madder than the Alexeyev's."

"We'll look after you. Is there a turf war going on?"

"I'm no' saying a thing. I want my lawyer."

"You don't need a lawyer. We haven't arrested you."

"I want a lawyer here while I speak to you."

"Someone call Angus Runcie." Shona didn't think she could take much more of this. She couldn't move for dodgy lawyers this week. She felt like chopping the lawyers and the chief up and feeding them to the wild pigs.

Chick was a lot more forthcoming with Angus in the room. They had to practically promise to protect his descendants for the next three hundred years though. Shona couldn't work out why he was bothering. She couldn't think of anyone alive who would want to procreate with Chic. He was all Brylcreemed hair and flash suit. The type of bloke who gave you the creeps just by being in the room.

"So Chick, what do you know about Bogdan?"

"He's more of a bampot than Jimmy McTaggart and the Alexeyev's rolled into one."

"Is there a turf war going on?"

"And some. Him and the Russians are trying to outdo each other."

"Did Angel work for either of them?"

"I've nae clue. He must have been working for someone though, as he was too stupid to go it alone."

"Where does Petrescu hang out?"

"The word on the street is that he's taken over The Jungle. It was him renamed it Lucifer's."

"Thanks Chic. You've been helpful. Would you like a lift back?"

"No. I'd like a cell for a few nights so that everyone thinks I've been arrested."

"No worries. Charles Anderson I'm arresting your for Interfering with a Police Investigation. Anything—"

"What, I haven't withheld anything. I've just helped you."

"You omitted to tell us about a person who was dealing drugs. We'll have to keep you in a cell for a few days until we find you innocent."

Chick's body relaxed so much he nearly fell from the chair.

"Take him to a cell and get him some grub from the canteen. He deserves something decent."

"What's Lucifer's? That's a new one on me," asked Shona. "I should think with a name like Lucifer's, Bodgan would have a pusher called Angel though."

"It's only been Lucifer's for a couple of weeks," said Nina. "It's a new nightclub."

"Have any of you been there?"

Jason and Roy looked a bit shifty.

"No' me. I'm getting into my pyjamas when the nightclubs get going."

"You could go in your onesie, Peter," said Jason.

"I'll have you running around the block in your onesie if you give me any more of your cheek."

"It looks like we've got another visit to a nightclub in our very near future." She took in Peter's panicked expression. "You're excused Peter. Everyone else is going."

Cheers erupted.

"Go get your clubbing gear on and get back here at 2100."

17

The entrance to the nightclub was down a dark alley and hard to find.

"You'd think they'd want a nightclub to be found," said Iain.

"It's Lucifer's innit. The Prince of Darkness himself. You wouldn't expect it to be lit up like a carnival ride, dimwit," said Roy.

"That's enough of the name calling. Remember we've all got guns and if anyone shoots you with theirs Roy, then I'm letting them off."

Roy, thinking he rather liked being alive, decided to keep his mouth shut..

"Take care with those weapons. Lose one and I'll send you down for a stretch myself."

"She eyed them up. They looked suitably decadent and ready to party. Nina looked particularly vampish in a skirt and top that left nothing to the imagination. Shona couldn't imagine where she was hiding her gun. Perfect, just what she needed for the special little job Shona had for her.

"Let's do this, Let's partyyyyy," said Shona for the benefit of the clubbers pushing past.

They tumbled into the club chattering, women's voices high, on excitement and life. Shona was impressed and thought she might nominate them for the Oscars. Inside it was as dark as hell. There were imitation fires throughout, which seemed to be the main light. Painted demons in cages, lit by a single red bulb, thrashed around under the weight of eternal torment. The dance floor had dark red lights and nothing else.

The writhing bodies, dancing to the pulsating music, completed the image that they were in hell. This being Dundee's newest and hottest nightclub, the place was packed. Shona thought she might really have died and gone to hell.

"Bogdan shouldn't be that hard to find," she yelled into Roy's ear. "You and the boys try to locate him. Pretend your eyeing up the birds."

The boys left and the girls joined the maelstrom on the dance floor. It turned out all they could do was writhe as there was little room to do anything else. The boys returned and dragged them off the dance floor.

"Over in the corner on a slightly raised dias. He's watching the room," said Jason.

"Let's get ourselves over there. Nina, you're the advance party. Get over there and strut your stuff. Have you got your gun?" She still wasn't sure Nina was carrying.

"All present and correct. Don't you worry," said Nina.

By the time they arrived Nina had the man practically begging at her feet. She had a gun at his throat, but it didn't seem to be bothering him. Shona could well imagine what Nina had been saying to him. Before he knew it he had several more guns in strategic places around his person. Shona had hers somewhere which fast cooled his ardour.

Shona flashed her ID card, "You're coming with us. We need to ask you a few questions."

He was bundled out of the club and into a waiting unmarked vehicle. She gave the nod and several more police cars appeared as if by magic. The officers jumped out and entered the club. Operation Drug Hell was now in process.

"You can all knock off now. See you tomorrow."

"I'm not knocking off. I've got clubbing gear on. I'm off out," said Nina.

"Me too." The others were in agreement.

It looked like her work was having a night out. Shona made her excuses and grabbed a taxi to take her home. She'd had enough clubbing for one night.

18

"I'm a' ahent like the coo's tail," said Peter as he dashed through the door to the squad room the next morning.

"Speak English for heavens sake. What have cows tails got to do with anything?"

"I'm all behind like the cow's tail. In other words I'm late."

"I can see that. I've not got time for witticisms. There are dead bodies to be seen to and pieced together. There's also a Romanian bad guy to interview."

"Where's everyone else."

"That's a good question. After their wild night they're probably still in bed. I'm off to buy bacon rolls. Phone them and tell them to get out of their pits."

"That's a job I'll relish."

They ate their rolls and had an accompanying beverage before going to tackle Bogdan. Shona decided he could stew for a bit longer. She was just in the mood for torturing criminals.

She grabbed a couple of PC's in case the tank disguised as Bogdan, decided to play up.

Suitably fortified with food and caffeine, it was time to interrogate Bogdan. His lawyer had also appeared ruining Shona's good mood.

"Interview with Bogdan Petrescu, DI Shona McKenzie, DS Peter Johnston and Angus Runcie in attendance. Right, Mr.—"

"Why you arrest me. I do nothing."

"I beg to differ. It would seem from last night's raid you're running a drug emporium from your nightclub."

"Drugs? I know nothing of drugs. Not me."

"You own the place sunshine, so you're to blame."

"You can't treat my client like this. He is an upstanding citizen." Shona treated Runcie in her usual fashion by totally ignoring him.

"What's is sunshine? Is raining outside," said Bogdan.

"You're the owner. They're your drugs. Is that simple enough for you? Do you know a man named Gabriel LaShawn, or Angel LaShawn?"

"I not know him."

"I find that hard to believe. I've heard otherwise."

"Why you persecute me. Left Romania to get away from that. No persecution in Scotland. I have rights."

"What gives you the impression I am persecuting you? I'm only asking a few questions."

He looked a bit addled. Shona was convinced he was as deadly as a viper and the confusion was all an act.

"Do you know Gregor and Stephan Alexeyev?"

"They are Russian garbage. I not speak of them." He spat a huge globule into the corner, narrowly missing one of the constables.

Shona leaned in close and said, "Do that again in my station and I'll sew your lips together."

Petrescu roared and tried to stand up. His rise to the vertical was prevented by the burly uniforms and Peter.

"Sit down, now, and answer my questions. How do you know the Alexeyevs?"

"You not hear? Why should I speak to you?"

"Because if you don't it will look very like you're hiding something. Answer the question."

"What question?"

Shona, her face red turned towards Runcie. "Instruct your client to answer my bloo–" She took a deep breath. "To answer my question."

Runcie's eyes narrowed, but he did as Shona asked. "Everyone know them. Dangerous men."

"From what I've heard, you're just as bad."

"I will not let you say this." His black eyes blazed fire and reminded Shona of Lucifer himself. The bewildered mask had slipped showing the true power of the man underneath.

"We're keeping you here until we do a bit more digging."

"You can't keep my client without charge."

"Thank you for reminding me. Bogdan Petrescu I am placing you under arrest for being concerned in the supply of a controlled drug."

"This is outrageous," said the ever predictable Runcie.

"Not as outrageous as the fees you'll charge him to get out of this mess. Take him away boys."

By the time they had finished the rest of the team had appeared. She asked the DC's to join her in the briefing room.

"Your lateness this morning was both unprofessional and unacceptable."

"Sorry, Ma'am. We had a late night." Roy couldn't look her in the eye.

"The lateness of your night, or otherwise, is not my concern. The lateness of your morning is. I will not have a repeat of this. Do I make myself clear?"

"Yes, Ma'am." Three simultaneous murmurs and the boys shuffled out the door.

Shona invited the female sergeants to join her in her office.

"I cannot tell you how disappointed I am in the pair of you. As sergeants you should be setting an example. If this happens again you will both be disciplined."

"Sorry, Ma'am. You're right." Even Nina was short

of a witty comeback.

Shona left her chastened team to it. She hurried round to the courthouse and paid a visit to Sheriff Struthers.

"Knowing you this isn't a social call, Shona."

"Got it in one. I need a warrant to search Bogdan Petrescu's gaff."

"You're a brave woman if you're going after him. I'll write it with pleasure." He moved to a filing cabinet and withdrew a sheet of paper. "You might want to speak to uniform as well. They'll have a list of his known associates. I've had a few through here."

"You're a scholar and a gent." With which kind words Shona took the proffered warrant and dashed out the door.

When she returned to the station the others were hard at it at their desks.

"Come on, we're off on a shout." The speed of response told Shona that her earlier words had hit their mark. Good job or she'd be lacking a team.

19

Bogdan's gaff was a huge house out in middle of nowhere, Angus. It had what seemed like a million acres of land around it, all enclosed by an electric fence.

"With a place as well secured as this he's either right about the persecution in Romania, or he's got something to hide," said Shona.

"I'd bet a months fag money on the fact he's got a lot to hide," said Peter.

"I'm not taking you up on it." She moved forward. "Let me at that security lock. A couple of minutes staring and one minute fumbling and the gates slid open.

"I swear you were robbing at your mother's knee," said Peter.

"The Professors in Oxford know all sorts. They were happy to teach me when I was there with my dad."

"Why would a bunch of academics know how to pick locks, Ma'am?" asked Jason. "They taught us a bit of that in the Army, but I'm not up to your standards."

"You'd be amazed what they get up to in Oxford. It's not all gentle dreaming spires."

They moved up the long driveway, scanning the area for movement. There was none. They rang the front door and not a sound was heard. Another ring brought no one scurrying to open the door. Shona repeated her trick with the lock. She failed.

"That's some sophisticated lock they've got on there. Use the battering ram."

Jason fetched it from the car and, with Peter's help,

expertly applied it to the lock. The door flew open and Peter and Jason jumped for cover. They needn't have bothered as there wasn't a soul in sight.

"Looks like Bogdan's warned them we were coming. Angus Runcie probably had a lot to do with it." The house was huge, the search took hours, and nothing came of it. Nothing to link Bogdan to any illgotten gains. They arrested his computers and took them home like the spoils of war. Apart from that all they got from their visit was a freezing cold trip to the boondocks. And in the case of most of the team an even bigger appetite.

Shona gave them time to grab something to eat and drink. The team dying of malnutrition and dehydration wasn't a good look. Whilst they had their noses in the feedbag she took a coffee and a sausage roll to her office. Sitting on her desk was a large envelope. She tore it open. It contained the DNA results for limb number 3. It was from another, as yet, unidentified body. The good news, if that is what it could be called, was they now had names for the two women who were missing the limbs numbered 1 and 2. They were both from Dundee. This was surprising given the leg that was found some distance from the City. One was Anya Peirs and the other Daisy Murray. She called the team to the briefing room. Their tea break was over.

"Roy, have you got an update on the research I asked you to do on Bertram Peirs?"

"He seems to be fairly mild mannered. In a few clubs but none that would give us cause for concern. Used to have a licence to keep dangerous animals but that's long gone out of date. A couple of incidents with past girlfriends who reported him for roughing them up. The charges were dropped though."

"Good work. Nina, you and I are going to visit Bertram and break the news about his wife's death. Roy, can you crack open our Romanian's computers and see what you can find."

"If there's a speck of dust on the innards, you'll know about it."

"I'm talking about information, not spring cleaning."

"It was a joke. I..."

He saw Shona's glazed look and said, "Will do, Ma'am."

"Abigail and Peter could you break the news to Daisy's parents? Interview them as well."

"You got it," said Abigail.

"Jason, do some searches on both women and see if they have anything in common. Roy will give you some tips."

"What about me?" said Iain.

"Dust Petrescu's computers for any prints. See if any of them are in the system."

She looked around the room. "Why is everyone still here?"

The team leapt up and disappeared in record breaking time. After turning up late they didn't want to give the boss any more room for complaint.

20

Bertram Peirs was at home once more. Shona was beginning to wonder if he did any work. His house was tastefully decorated. Shona could tell antiques at a glance and there were several highly expensive ones in here. Her mother's passion sometimes paid off as she had taught Shona to tell a fake from the real deal. There was no shortage of money in this household.

"I've told you everything I know."

Shona kept her voice low and soothing. She was about to tell the poor man about his wife's demise after all. "Mr Peirs, we appreciate that fact. I am sorry but we are here to inform you that one of the bodies we have found is that of your wife."

"What? I thought she'd gone back to Romania."

That's the first we've heard of it thought Shona.

"If you thought that why did you report her missing?"

"I didn't want anyone thinking I'd done anything to her."

"That's a bit of a strange conclusion to come to, Mr Peirs."

"I watch television."

Yeah, that and the fact you've been arrested a couple of times for beating up women.

"The last time we were here you asked if she was dead. You seem to have changed your mind."

"I haven't. I don't know what to think. She is dead," the man blurted out.

Shona changed tack. She wanted to keep him

muddled. "What do you do for a living Mr Peirs?"

"I buy and restore antique furniture."

"Yet you're always at home."

"I work from home."

Considering he always looked well scrubbed this was hard to believe. She glanced at his hands. They were calloused which would give credence to his story.

"Did your wife work?"

"I answered all these questions when she went missing."

"It's important that I ask questions. I appreciate it's difficult but we need to catch your wife's killer."

"She was a barmaid."

"Which pub?"

"The Rabbie."

Shona looked at Nina who said, "The Robert Falcon Scott on the Perth Road."

Shona shifted focus again. "You've been arrested a couple of times for beating up a couple of ex girlfriends."

"Wha... What? Those charges were dropped."

"After both women had an unexpected windfall. Very convenient for you."

"It was. I'll admit I got a wee bit carried away, but I'm different now."

"You've got a history of violence against women, and now a dead wife. It doesn't look any different to me."

"I didn't kill my wife."

"We haven't any more questions at the moment. Don't leave Dundee. If you even think about leaving you'll be banged up in one of my cells quicker than you can say escape."

"I've nothing to hide so I won't be going anywhere."

"We'll be re-examining what you did to those

women as well."

She left Bertram glaring at her with evil blazing from his eyes.

"Do you believe him?" asked Nina as they drove home.

"I have to for the moment. We can't exactly put an electronic tag on him."

"If you think he's a flight risk you could nab him and chuck him in a cell for a few days."

"Go easy cowboy. How are things with you and Mr Charismatic the lawyer?"

"It never got going. Turns out he's married."

"What? And he didn't tell you?"

"He did tell me. He's separated at the moment but I get the impression he wants to get back with her. Anyway I've moved on. I'm going out with Gerry McLachlan now."

"The bloke who owns the car showrooms."

"No. He's about a hundred. It's his grandson. He's got a huge—"

"Nina!"

"—car. I was going to say car. Top of the range Merc."

"Yeah right. Remember we're friends and I know you."

They hadn't managed to get back to the station when the duty sergeant called. With the wonders of hands free and voice control Shona was able to answer.

"There's been a woman's torso found in Templeton Woods, Ma'am."

"Tell them I'm on my way. Have Iain Barrow meet me there. Peter's out on a visit. Send him in my direction as well. Leave the others be."

21

As they drove up the road to the woods an ambulance flew past, sirens blaring. Templeton woods was a beauty spot on the outskirts of Dundee. It covered one hundred and forty nine acres. Shona had no clue as to how they were going to find the right area. Her sense of direction could be described as lacking, but only by those kindly disposed to her. Everyone else said it was dire. Nina, thankfully, was better at map reading than Shona.

"Get Sandy to text me the coordinates."

Sandy, the duty sergeant, complied and Nina was using a fancy app on her phone within minutes. They were heading in the right direction before they could say crime scene.

Shona was in awe. "How come you know so much about this?"

"I go hill walking. You don't think I've got a pair of Hunter Wellies in my car for no reason."

Nina was currently employing Shona's wellies as her Christian Louboutan's weren't quite up to the task. Shona's shoes, on the other hand were eminently suitable. Designer shoes didn't really go with Chino's and a leather jacket.

It had started to rain by the time they arrived. The type of rain, too mean to give it's all. Yet the wind whipped it into a needle sharp frenzy which pierced both skin and clothes in equal measure. There was a huge area surrounded by crime scene tape and, for once, no gawkers. In fact, apart from the police, there was no one at all.

"Was the torso found by the police?" asked Shona.

"No," replied Sergeant Muir. "An old couple."

"Where are they?"

"Ninewells. The woman collapsed with the shock. She was carted off in an ambulance."

"Can we go in?"

"Yes. PC Gevers will take you to the right spot."

"Lead on Brian."

As they arrived at the scene Shona saw something leaning against a tree. Something out of place which should not be at any one of her crime scenes.

"Where did that spade come from? I jolly well hope that no one has been digging here."

Brian jumped at her sharp tone.

"Ma'am, the spade belongs to the witnesses. They were using a metal detector and started digging when they got a hit."

Shona wondered what had set off the metal detector.

"Thanks. We'll take it from here. The less people trampling around the better." Her smile softened the words and Brian left with his confidence in her sunny nature restored.

Shona and Nina pulled on gloves to match the overshoes they already had on their feet. They stared critically around them. The torso hadn't been there long, even Shona could tell that. There was some degree of decomposition but not much. Despite being partially eaten there were definitely breasts so probably a woman. However, Shona knew enough never to assume. If you took gynaecomastia, or male breasts into consideration, then the gender could be wrong. It could also be a man undergoing gender reassignment. As they could only see part of the torso it was difficult to say definitively. These thoughts ran through her mind as though it were attached to a computer.

"What a way to end up," said Nina. The thought of what this poor woman, or man, had gone through had batted her usually sunny nature out of the field.

"It sends shivers down my spine just thinking about it."

Both Iain and Mary arrived at the same time.

"Let me at it," said Iain, as he took the cap of the cameral lens. He got to work with the most expensive camera the department had ever owned. The price made Shona's eye's water and shoved the chief's blood pressure up several points on the scale.

"Another bit of your jigsaw, Shona," said Mary. She was eyeing the scene up keenly and pointing out to Iain where the photos should be taken. Mary took multitasking to a whole new level.

"Here's hoping. So far we've three jigsaws. I'm hoping this isn't a fourth."

"Knowing you anything is possible."

Shona had to agree. Shed loads of dead bodies and out of the ordinary cases did seem to follow her around.

Nina had been dispatched to find coveralls. She returned fully kitted out and Mary and Shona soon joined her. All three got to work brushing leaves and wet earth from around the torso. Iain was taking photos at strategic intervals. It was a slow process as everything had to be documented and put into specimen bags. After roughly an hour of laborious search they found the reason for the ping of the metal detector. A gold locket lay buried a few inches below the body. A specimen bag was produced and the locket dropped in. By the time they had finished, the wolves were baying at the door.

"Are these dogs always so noisy? You'd think they'd be better trained than that," said Shona.

"They're just telling you they're eager to get on

with the job," called one of the handlers.

"Well they don't have to shout so loudly."

"The minute they start they will be as quiet as mice, Ma'am."

"Let them do the wider area. If nothing else it'll shut them up."

The handlers let the dogs have at it and Shona said her goodbyes to Mary.

"I'll ring you when I get back," said Mary. "I've got an update for you."

Before she left Shona sent Peter up to Ninewells Hospital to find out how their witnesses were and whether they were up to being interviewed.

22

By the time Shona returned to the Gulags the rain had let up. Adanna Okifor was also parked on her doorstep. Well, the front hallway anyway.

"How come you're here and not hounding my crime scene?"

"I knew you wouldn't let me anywhere near it and it's a bit wet out there."

"I thought reporters were made of sterner stuff than that. Would you like a coffee to heat you up?"

Shona was being sarcastic but Adanna said, "Black with four sugars."

Feeling wet, miserable and charitable Shona decided to grant the request. She took the reporter through to her office.

"Where do you think this case is going then," asked Adanna once she'd taken a gulp of her scalding hot beverage. The temperature didn't seem to bother her.

"I offered you a coffee not the inside scoop."

"You must have some idea."

"The only place it seems to be going is all over Scotland. We're looking into a couple of things but it's going nowhere."

They gazed into their drinks for a few minutes as though they would see the answers in the steam. Then Shona said, "You lot are always nosing into other people's business. Have you heard anything?"

"There's nothing on the street. One snippet of info did come my way. It looks like one of Bogdan Petrescu's boys is running around with crossbows. One of our photographers accidently snapped him."

"We need that photo."

Adanna pulled it from her voluminous red handbag. "It's all yours."

"And you didn't think to tell me this before now."

"I brought it straight over. Thought I'd chance my hand at getting the skinny from you first." A large smile lit up her face.

"Much as I'd love to chat, I've an investigation to run. Bye now." Adanna was dismissed in the same fashion as the chief dismissed Shona.

The team were still out and about on official duties. Shona had a couple of calls from her contemporaries in other areas. She took advantage of the lull to return them. She then wished she hadn't. They now had one more severed leg and a severed head to deal with. These were in Perth and Lochgoilhead respectively. Shona had no clue where Lochgoilhead was so she opened up the police mapping software. It was harder to use than Google Maps but a lot more secure. The police might want Google to keep records of where everyone went but wanted their own privacy. Double standards? Absolutely. All is fair in love and crime fighting.

It appeared it was close to Inveraray, the site of the initial find, although not on the same route. It was only a dog leg off though so doable in one trip.

"The killer's trying to put us off the scent." There was nothing more than a cold cup of coffee around to hear her insightful words.

Perth had agreed to manage the crime scene their end. They were going to video everything and send it through. The only problem with having a Mobile Incident Team in a case like this was that they wouldn't be able to investigate for travelling. Maybe the killer was bright enough to realise that.

Gordon Bessant in the Highlands and Islands agreed to do the same.

"Anything you need, Shona, just let me know. I've heard it's tough down in Dundee at the moment."

"You have no idea. Are Benbecula looking for a DI?"

"That would be my job, so hands off. Plus Highlands and Islands wouldn't want you. Too many dead bodies to deal with. The nearest we get to dead bodies is a whale washing up on the beach. We've not had one since 1967 when Jimmy Murthie got drunk and died of exposure on his way home from the pub."

With that cheery word he hung up and left her to her thoughts. These thoughts were as coherent as a whirlwind, tornado and hurricane all rolled into one. She took a deep breath and grabbed a piece of paper and a pen. What did they already know? Going through things systematically calmed her mind down and at least she had an up-to-date timeline of what was going on. She moved to the briefing room and wrote the timeline on the board. Peter came strolling through the door with the others in tow. They'd all managed to grab hot drinks and cakes before they found her.

"Glad, to see you've got your priorities straight."

"Aye, we have. It's colder than a penguin's a... behind out there," said Peter.

He handed her a coffee and Abigail handed her a cake. Just the thing to get the mass between her ears working thought Shona.

"Did you find anything at the scene."

"I've lost something. All the feeling in my hands and feet," said Peter.

"Stop whining. You've been a copper for years you should be used to it by now. Will someone answer my question?"

"The usual sweet papers, fag ends, dog muck,

and..." Nina paused.

"Spit it out. I'm going grey here."

"And the remnants of some brown wrapping paper and string."

"Same perpetrator then."

This was all very well thought Shona, but how were they going to catch him or her.

"Did Mary come back with you lot?"

"She left just before us," said Abigail.

Shona stood up. "I'm off to pay her a visit."

"Shona, I've barely got time to breath with all the work you're chucking in my direction."

Despite this she poured Shona a coffee and indicated she should sit down.

"Sorry. You said you needed to talk," said Shona.

"I'll cut to the chase. Someone who knew what they were doing chopped off the limbs. This was no hatchet job."

"Who would know how to do that?"

"Surgeon. Butcher. Pathologist."

"Please don't go down the pathologist route. I couldn't bear to interview you guys again."

"I'm glad about that. I've not got time for us to be spending in useless interviews. Let's just say it's no one from my team."

"What about your trainee with the dogging habit."

"Cleaned up his act and now an upstanding, fully employed, member of my team."

"So that leaves us with a surgeon or a butcher. I'd leave the surgeon out of the equation if it weren't for the likes of Harold Shipman or Beverley Allitt. Any other trade that might know about chopping up bodies?"

"A vet? They've been known to chop off limbs for an extortionate fee."

"What about a woodcutter? They're pretty handy

with an axe."

"I'd say it was someone with a good knowledge of anatomy."

"I'll leave you to it then. I'm sure you've more bodies to be cutting in to."

"Slow down. I'm not finished yet."

Shona thumped back down into the chair.

"All your body parts were frozen before they were dumped in the ground."

"Frozen. So we're looking for someone who is expert at chopping bodies up and has a freezer large enough to store body parts. That'll be you then, Mary."

"Feel free to check every last freezer. The only body parts there are legit."

"It's likely a butcher then," said Nina when Shona broke the news to the team.

"Yep. Seems so. Remind me. How many butchers are there in Dundee?"

"Hundred's, Ma'am. But you'd be best trying Big Brenda's first," said Peter.

"Who's Big Brenda?"

"A butcher of this Parish. She's so big she could hold a couple of cows under each arm and still have room for her handbag."

"Why does everyone in Dundee have a nickname? Where is her butcher's shop?"

"Lamb's, at the bottom of the Hilltown," said Abigail. Despite being new to the city she seemed to know more about it than Shona did.

"Are you having me on? A butcher with the name of Lamb."

"No it's gen up," said Roy. "It's been there for years. It was her father, Wee Eric's, shop. He was called Wee Eric because his dad—"

"Roy, shut up. I'm not interested in Brenda's family

tree." She thought for a minute. "Peter, why do we need to talk to Brenda? We can't arrest her for being a butcher and a bit on the large side."

"She was caught a few years ago selling horse meat burgers as the real McCoy. They fined her an obscene amount of money and checked every nook and cranny of the shop. They said she could re-open but they kept an eye on her for a couple of years. They've stopped paying her much attention now so she could have diversified."

"I've a sudden urge to go vegetarian. Peter, you come with me. We're going to have a wee word with Brenda."

"You might want to take a couple of strong lads as well. I'm no' joking when I say Brenda's a big lass."

"Roy. Jason. You're on. Let's go."

Shona stood and stared at the vision in front of her. Almost seven foot tall and about five times that in stones she would have given Mount Everest a run for its money. She had upper arms that were larger, stronger and tougher than the huge hams she was selling.

"What are you gawping at? Do you no' see many women?"

Shona couldn't seem to formulate a response.

"Either buy something or shove off. I've just had some nice peh's in just now."

Shona had learned that peh's, or pies in English, were shortcrust pastry filled with spicy mince and a bucket full of liquid grease. They were a particular favourite of Dundonians who could scoff several in one go. She managed to show her ID card and said, "DI Shona McKenzie of Dundee CID. Can we have a word?"

"I've not done nothing. You can't say I have. I know my rights."

You and every other lowlife in the city thought Shona. Nothing between your ears but you're an expert in the law.

"We're not saying that you've done anything. We would just like to ask you a few questions."

"I'm no saying anything without my lawyer being here. I've dealt with the pigs before. You'll frame me for something."

"We'll do no such thing, Brenda."

"It's Big Brenda. My cousin's wee Brenda."

"For heaven's sake I don't need to know about your familial history. I just want to ask a few questions."

"You what?"

Shona changed tack. "I've a warrant here to look inside your freezers."

"No way." Brenda picked up a meat cleaver.

She suddenly found herself facing four Glock 17's. "Put the weapon down."

Brenda raised the cleaver higher and threw it in Shona's direction. Shona neatly sidestepped the poorly aimed hatchet and the others jumped forward. Big Brenda decided to use her fists one of which made contact with Jason who immediately bent over and fell to his knees. Peter made his weapon ready and aimed it a Big Brenda's head. "Give it up now, Brenda. Wee Eric would be ashamed of you."

At the mention of her long dead dad the fight seemed to go out of Brenda. They shoved her into some handcuffs and left her to Peter and Jason. Shona took Roy to search the freezers. There was nothing resembling human anatomy in there. Or anything untoward come to that.

Jason had recovered enough to take Brenda back to the station with Roy. There wasn't enough room in the car so they'd called for a van. On the way back with Peter,

Shona asked, "How did you know Brenda would calm down so quickly if you brought her dad up?"

"Eric and me were pals. He doted on his lassie and Brenda doted on him."

The thought of anyone doting on the Mount Everest lookalike was not something Shona could picture. Given Brenda's reaction it was obviously true.

23

Brenda wasn't quite such a docile lamb on her entrance to the station. In fact she was just the opposite. The fiercest lions would have quaked and turned tail when faced with Brenda in a mood. Shona, unfortunately, did not have that luxury.

"Shut up woman," shouted Shona. It had no effect. Shona couldn't even shout it in Brenda's ear because she was about a foot shorter than their prisoner.

Shona ran to her office, grabbed the thickest file she could find, and headed towards the interview room. She slammed the file on the table with such force it made the table rattle. It also had the intended effect of shutting Brenda up. Brenda eyed the file from half closed eyelids.

"That's not mine. I've not been in that much trouble."

"No it isn't. But if you keep shouting the odds in my station yours will soon be as thick as this."

"You arrested me for nothing."

"I arrested you for assaulting a police officer."

"I was provoked."

There was a knock at the door and Nina ushered Henry in.

"Why are you interviewing my client before I arrived," asked Henry in a voice that could freeze oil.

"We're not interviewing her. We haven't got started yet."

Having reasserted his right to be alpha male, Henry smiled. Mr Charismatic was back.

Shona didn't have time for power games so she continued. "Miss lamb, you've only made things worse for yourself."

At the sound of the name, Miss Lamb, Shona could hear choking sounds from Roy. Despite agreeing with him she threw him a withering look.

"You know a lot about butchery. Is that right Miss Lamb?"

"Aye and it's not a crime to be a butcher. I don't need the qualifications of Mr Fancy Pants here," she indicated her Lawyer, "to know that much."

"That's absolutely right. But it gives you certain skills, shall we say."

"What?"

"You know how to carve up bodies."

"Of course I do." Brenda had a look in her eye that said Shona was a dimwit.

Don't look at me like that sunshine. You've dug yourself into a hole that is full of carved up body parts thought Shona

"Would carving up a human body be much different?"

Brenda's eyebrows moved closer together. This was some feat as they were already meeting in the middle. "What? What? You're not saying I carved up thon arms and legs that have been found? That wisnae me. No way."

The file was re-employed to good effect.

"Stop shouting. The last time I heard I am not deaf."

"You cu—"

Shona had had just about enough of this. She shouted even louder than Brenda. "No swearing either."

"This is a cop shop no' a nursery."

"I'm perfectly well aware of that. But it's my cop shop and I say no shouting or swearing. Now, we are not accusing you of anything. We are just asking you if someone with butchery training could carve up a human body?"

"I suppose they could. It wouldn't be much different."

"Including you. We've a warrant to go through your shop and freezers. My boys are busy doing that as we speak." Shona had dispatched Iain, Jason and Abigail back to the butcher's shop, where she hoped they were busy being meticulous.

"I keep telling you. I've stopped doing dodgy deals. I'm a new woman."

"That new that you threatened us with a meat cleaver. You'll be staying nice and cosy in our cells for a while, until you are seen in the sheriff's court."

"I'm losing money. You ba..."

She stopped short as Shona stood up.

"You'll be losing more than that love. You'll be losing your liberty," said Shona as she picked up her file and walked out the door.

Do you know how much blood there is in a butcher's shop?" asked Iain on his return.

"Not exactly but I'd hazard a guess as to it being a lot." said Shona.

"Far too much. It's taken us hours."

"Stop moaning."

"You'd be moaning if you'd spent the last few hours in a butcher's freezer."

"Grab a coffee to heat you up and get on with it. You're a crack CID team not a bunch of poodles."

"Where do we go from here?" asked Abigail when they gathered in the briefing room.

"Good question but I'm dashed if I know the answer. Two cases which are going nowhere. Let's take them one at a time. Jason, what did your search on the two women throw up?"

"At first glance they've nothing in common. There's very little out there on Daisy. From her Facebook profile it would seem she's unmarried and looking for a man. She did join a couple of dating sites and has been out on a few dates."

"Find out the names of the men she dated. We'll have a conversation with them."

"I think it might have been women, Ma'am."

"Who cares. Just find them. Anything else on her?"

"According to social media it would appear she was in to reading romance and knitting."

"That would tie up with what her parents told us," said Peter. "She preferred to be at home reading. Didn't go out much. They didn't say anything about dating sites, or any dating at all. We asked if she had a boyfriend and they said no. She'd only had one boyfriend and it broke up after a few weeks."

"What about Anya?"

"Being married she wasn't on any dating sites. As Bertram said, she was from Romania."

Roy took over. "I looked into any links between her and Bogdan. There was nothing. They're from completely different areas of Romania. No familial links. Don't appear to have any friends in common. I even looked into possible importing of illegal immigrants, but that didn't pan out either."

"Did she have any friends we could talk to?"

"She was friendly with another couple of Eastern European brides."

"Roy, you're on computer duty. Dig deeper. Go wherever you have to and I'll square it with the chief."

"You've got it." Roy bounded off full of restless energy and enthusiasm.

"That laddie wears me out," said Peter.

"Me too. Nina, ring up the dating agencies and get

the names of the men, or women, Daisy dated. Abigail contact Anya's friends and bring them in for a chat. Make sure to tell them they're not in trouble we just need to find out more about her."

"Peter, you're with me. We're off to visit the Rabbie."

"How come you pair get to go to the pub?" asked Nina.

"Because I'm the boss and I say so. Besides if I sent you to a pub you'd be dating the barman by teatime."

"I don't think even Nina would be dating this one," said Peter.

24

The Rabbie was a scruffy little pub on the Perth Road. Despite it's downmarket demeanour there was a fair scattering of punters. These were a mixture of old men and what looked like students.

"How come this place seems so popular?"

"Cheap booze and cheap food. They undercut everyone else."

Peter knew more about Dundee than Shona would ever know. She was dreading the day that he retired. It wouldn't so much leave a hole in the team, as a gaping chasm. The interior, with walls painted dark mustard by cigarette smoke, shouted that the pub hadn't been updated in about fifty years. The man behind the bar looked like he'd been working there for about a hundred years. No wonder Peter thought Nina wouldn't be interested. Mind you, knowing Nina.

"Morning, Alex. How's business?" said Peter. Shona let him take the lead.

"No' bad. Would you like a pint?" He looked at Shona. "You look like a whisky drinker to me."

Shona was impressed. She put her hand out and shook Alex's rough one. "Detective Inspector Shona McKenzie. We'd better not drink. We're driving."

"That zero driving limit you lot brought in is killing business. Good thing though. I took folks car keys away in here and only gave them back if they were fit to drive." He paused then, "She your boss." The old man looked over at Peter, without letting go of Shona's hand.

Peter nodded.

"Good for you lass. Somebodies got to keep this old rascal under control." He returned her hand.

"We've heard Anya Peirs worked here," said Peter.

"Aye, that's right. Three nights a week. But she disappeared on me."

That's funny thought Shona. She'd got the impression from her husband that Anya worked full time. She made a note on her iPhone to chase it up.

"I'm sorry to have to tell you she's dead."

"That's a shame that is. She was a nice lassie. Struggled with English sometimes, but a hard worker."

Shona was willing to bet it was Scottish she struggled with and her English was perfectly good.

"Did you ever have any problems with her at all?" asked Shona.

"Never. One of my best barmaids. The punters loved her. She was a grafter and strong. My was she strong. She could carry a barrel better than any man."

"Do you know what her relationship with her husband was like?"

"She never said much about him. He came in a few times., Had a quick word with her, then sat and drank a couple of pints of Export. Never took his eyes off her. No' right in the head if you ask me."

Love or obsession? Shona made a mental note to follow that up.

"Did anyone else come in to see her?"

"Some friends occasionally. No one to speak of."

"Male or female friends?" asked Shona.

"Always women. I'm no' sure that husband of hers would tolerate men sniffing round."

Shona handed over her business card. "If you think of anything let me know."

"Aye, right you are."

The team were hard at work when they returned.

"Got anything yet, Roy?"

"No." He continued with his furious tapping without looking up. Shona didn't even want to think about what he was up to on the web.

"Nina, have we got those names yet."

"They're not giving them up without a fight. The local squad are taking a warrant round and informing them it would be in their best interests to phone me back."

"Good work. Let me know the minute you've got them."

"I don't think it will be tonight. It's nearly 8 o'clock."

"Good point. Abigail, have you managed to get hold of Anya's friends?"

"Yep. They're both at work so I said they could come in first thing in the morning. They've agreed to come at 0900."

"You can all scurry home to your nearest and dearest. I'll see you here at 0800."

"What? Surely—"

"Can it, Roy. I'm not interested. Any more arguments and you can meet me here at 0700."

That pretty effectively shut him up.

Shona didn't have the energy for her nearest and dearest. Besides, by this stage Douglas would be putting Alice to bed. She could whisper sweet nothings in her beloved's ear another night she thought.

25

Furious meowing in her ear was not Shona's favourite way to be roused. The meowing seemed to indicate something other than Shakespeare's hunger.

"What's up moggy?" She glanced at the clock and switched on the light. She instantly regretted it. A bloody human finger lay on her duvet.

She screamed and the cat bolted. "Where did that come from," she yelled after the animal.

She left the bedroom to explore. Given what she'd just found she realised this was a really stupid move. Why have I never got a gun when I really need it? I'm bringing one home with me in future. She had, however, picked up a paper opener on her way from the bedroom. Not much of a weapon, but it was antique, heavy and looked like a knife. It was the best she could do given the circumstances.

She moved stealthily, turning on lights as she went. Not a soul in the flat other than her. The blood on her letterbox and doormat gave away the source. Someone had posted it through her door. Shivers rushed down her spine and ran screaming out to the rest of her body. The killer knew where she lived. Shaking, she picked up the phone and called the station. She then called Peter, Nina and Douglas.

"I need you at my house now," was all she said to each of them.

A squad car arrived within a few minutes, dispatched from the local station. Luckily Shona had kept enough of her wits about her to get dressed. She'd also managed to feed Shakespeare who was sulking in the kitchen. Her look quite clearly said, "Don't shoot the messenger."

Shona petted the cat. "Sorry kitty."

The coppers got to work making her flat, and the stairwell, into a crime scene.

"Don't step through the door she yelled when they knocked."

They stayed where they were as she opened the door.

"There's evidence on the floor and in my bedroom. We need to preserve it until my scene of crime officer arrives."

"Righty ho, Ma'am." The copper was far too cheerful for Shona's liking.

Douglas came hurtling up the stairs and was quite expertly stopped by a couple of officers. "You can't go any further, Sir."

"Do you know who I am?"

Before they could answer Shona shouted out through he doorway. "They know exactly who you are. They're acting on my instructions. No one comes in here until we've collected evidence."

"Even me?"

"Especially you. You should know better."

"What on earth have you been doing now, Ma'am. We can't leave you on your own for a minute." Peter had arrived, closely followed by a white faced Nina.

"Shona, thank goodness you're okay. I was thinking the worst all the way here," said Nina.

"I'm as a good as anyone can be who woke up to a bloody finger on their bed." She started shaking again and sat down on the hallway floor. Her stomach tightened to try to stop the dry heaves which were threatening her body.

"What. How did it get on your bed? Did somebody get in?" Douglas tied to break through again. His need to comfort Shona overpowered his usual good sense.

"No you don't, Sir. We'll arrest you if you try that again." The coppers guarding the doorway were firm.

"Relax. It doesn't look as if anyone broke in. I think it was posted through the door. Shakespeare bore his trophy to my room." Inane chatter was helping her focus and stopping her falling apart.

"Seriously, Shona, we didn't have any of this before you turned up." Peter's use of her first name was an indication of his level of anxiety.

"Well at least I keep things interesting," said Shona, a tremble in her voice.

"This is taking 'giving the police the finger' to the extreme," said Nina.

"That's dreadful even for you." Shona gave her a weak smile.

It seemed like hours but was probably only about twenty minutes before Iain arrived. Shona pulled herself together and was in charge of both the team, and her emotions, again.

"Iain, get this lot back down the stairs. You examine the stairwell. Nina and Peter, you can have a scout about outside." Iain turned to leave. "Not so fast. I need swabs and some specimen bags. Give me the fingerprint kit as well. They may have touched the inside of the letter box."

Douglas's mouth opened and Shona cut him off at the pass. I know you're the procurator fiscal and I'll brief you in due course. I also know you're my boyfriend, so hang around. I'll need you to hug me when this is over. With that she turned to her duties of collecting evidence.

26

The rest of the team were slack jawed when they heard what had been going on.

"How come you never called us? We miss all the fun," said Roy.

"Finding body parts in your bed isn't exactly what I would call fun," said Shona.

"The boss disnae want you lot seeing her in her nightie," said Peter.

"It's a bit late for that in my case," said Roy.

"Is there something we should know," said Abigail.

"Roy, tell them the real story. I'm off to brief the chief and there had better be a couple of bacon and egg rolls waiting for me on my return."

As she left she could see Peter handing Jason a twenty pound note. Blimey, they must feel sorry for me if Peter's opening his wallet, thought Shona. He was the quintessential miserly Scotsman.

As she thought the chief wasn't particularly upset by the fact she'd had a fright. He was more bothered about the chaos that seemed to surround his CID team.

"Every other chief in the country, no make that the whole of the UK, seems to have a crack team. Why did I get you lot."

"But, Sir—"

"I'm not finished. Can you not carry out an investigation without havoc ensuing?"

"But, Sir—"

"I don't want to hear any more of your

shenanigans. Try to get through the rest of this investigation in a professional manner. That will be all."

Shona left his office thinking it would be a good idea to chop his body up and feed him to the lions in Edinburgh zoo, never mind one quirky household cat. Why had she been landed with the worst chief inspector in the whole of the UK?

She rang down to Mary to make sure she'd received the finger. Mary reassured her that she had and said, "Just when I think things can't get any stranger you pull another one out of the hat. You certainly keep things lively, Ghengis."

No one seemed to give a toss about the fact she'd had a nasty shock. They were more interested in the fact she could collect dead bodies like a spotter collected trains. Oh well, she thought, at least I can't dwell on things for too long. When she arrived back at the office she was greeted by the sight of Doreen holding a couple of rolls piled high with sausage, bacon and egg. Shona fell on them like she'd just come off a hunger strike.

"She never brought the rest of us any," said Peter.

"The rest of you never had a fright like Shona. I wanted to make sure she got some nice hot, fresh food. Anyhow, you carted your own food off in paper bags."

"Guilty as charged."

"I can tell, Jason. You've got egg all over your face," said Shona. "Get yourself sorted out."

While Jason liberally applied a tissue and some spit, Shona turned to Roy. "Where are you up to with the connection between our dead women?"

"I've found nothing. They didn't even go to school together. Anya didn't come over here until about 3 months before she married Bertram. They appear to have nothing in common."

"Keep digging. Have the dating agency coughed up those names yet?"

"Not that I know of. I haven't had any calls as yet."

"I've had enough of this. They'll give them up meek as lambs when I speak to them." She stormed off to her office.

"Have the police served that warrant." She listened. "Give me those names now. You've a warrant which gives you specific instructions to hand them over to me." Another pause, "I'll hold whilst you look them up." After a ten minute wait listening to the most annoying music in the world she had four names in her hand.

"Nina," she called through the squad room door. Nina jumped to do her bidding. Get this lot in here." She handed the paper over. "I don't care if they're working. Tell them we'll send blue lights and handcuffs if they don't appear post haste."

Nina bent over her phone.

"Abigail, what time are Anya's friends coming in?"

"They should be here any minute now."

"You and Nina can interview them."

She looked over at Jason. "Have you got any injuries?"

He looked puzzled. "No, Ma'am."

"Good." She handed him the photo the reporter had given her. "Find out who this is."

"Where do I start?"

"For heavens sake, Jason. Use your loaf. Show the picture around. Start with uniform. He might be a petty crook and they know him."

Sorting her team out at times was like herding cats. She was sure she only had one nerve left and wasn't sure how long it would last out without snapping. Lack of sleep and the excess adrenaline wearing off had her exhausted.

The chief was waiting for her when she returned to the office.

"Shona, I've had a word with uniform and they're going to keep a close eye on your flats."

To say Shona was dumfounded would not have been so much an understatement as an excavation.

The chief continued, "You're going to have twenty four seven protection until this is over."

"Sir, it's going to be difficult to do my—"

"This is not up for discussion. It is my responsibility to protect you and I will do so even if I have to call in every favour I have every been owed."

"Thank you, Sir." Well I never. The old goat has a soft side after all, she thought.

She'd no sooner sat down than Douglas's kids materialised.

"Shona, daddy said we're going to take you out to tea tonight," said Alice. She was dancing from foot to foot, bunches swinging in time to her beat.

Rory had quite a different type of beat. He was listening to music on his brand new phone. He took his earphones out long enough to say, "What's up? Dad said you'd had a fright. You okay?"

"I'm absolutely peachy thanks, Rory. I can't come out to tea though. I've no clue what time I'll be knocking off."

"Daddy, said we could go to Nando's." Alice wasn't quite so bouncy now. Her lower lip was quivering.

"I'm sure he'll still take you." Shona ruffled her hair.

Face beaming, Alice said, "Good." The thought of spicy chicken had her back to her usual self.

At that, the man himself turned up. "Thomas has just been telling me he's got uniform keeping an eye on you."

"Did you arrange that?" Shona's tone could have frozen one of their corpses.

"No, but it's a good idea."

"No it flaming isn't. It's the worst idea I've ever heard. How am I meant to do my job with hangers on mirroring my every move?"

"You need to be safe."

"And you need to back off."

She glared at him until she heard a voice say, "Why are you being mean to each other. It's not nice to be mean."

Shona's voice softened, "Sorry Alice. You're right. Maybe you'd like to take the kids off for that meal now Douglas." Her voice was cheerful but her look told him this discussion was not over.

"God spare me from protective men," she said to Fagin, who had appeared in her office and was jumping up on her. "What are you doing here?" The pup cleaned her face with a long tongue, his tail wagging like he'd swallowed speed.

"Jock brought him in to see you," said Abigail, who'd followed the pup.

"Just what I needed, a man that loves me but doesn't tell me what to do. Do you think Jock would give him back."

"Not a chance. It's a match made in heaven."

By the time Fagin was returned to his owner he'd managed to nick a couple of sausages and was trailing someone's scarf behind him.

"You haven't managed to control his thieving then Jock."

"I think he's vying for the naughtiest dog in the world award. He's untrainable." Jock rubbed the dog's long ears. Fagin whined and put a paw on Jock's knee. Shona's heart melted and she swallowed against the lump that had appeared in her throat.

On Shona's return to her office she found that information had started to pour in, lending a certain sense of urgency. Up until now the case had seemed a little stale. Jason, had a possible hit on the man with the crossbow.

"Ally Cauldwell. He's a tuppenny ha'penny player who thinks he's a hard man. Attaches himself to whatever low life fancies himself as king of the hill at any given moment. He's been inside a couple of times for assault to injury."

"Sounds like a nice sort of chap. I think I'll invite him round for a cuppa and a wee chat. How do we find him?"

"Should be easy enough. He hangs out at Joey's a crappy little pub down near the docks. It should have been shut down years ago."

"So why is the landlord still plying his wares?"

"Because we know where to find the dregs of society if we ever need to haul them in."

"Go fetch him."

"You won't find him until about 9 o'clock."

"You, Roy and Iain can sort it out. I want him in a cell when I arrive tomorrow morning."

The next piece of information meant the game of human jigsaw had well and truly begun.

27

Shona slit open an envelope and pulled out the results of the DNA testing on the scattered body parts. The leg they'd found at Westmuir belonged to another female. As they'd taken DNA from the relatives of all the missing females they were able to identify her as Trisha Leyland. Shona's interest was further piqued on reading the next results. The leg found in Perth belonged to Anya Peirs, and the head belonged to Daisy Murray. The jigsaws were starting to take rudimentary shape. Someone was indeed playing a game of human treasure hunt. Her heart sank at the thought of how many more limbs would be found. If they were found. Andy, from uniform, interrupted her in her reverie.

"We've a missing person report come in. I thought you'd be interested as it's a female about the ages of your dead women."

"Thanks. What's her name?"

"Kylie Paterson."

"Are you able to do the initial investigation?"

"Will do. Anything special you want us to ask the next of kin?"

"Yep. Did she know Anya Peirs, Daisy Murray or Trisha Leyland?"

The plot definitely thickens, thought Shona. She knew in the very depth of her soul that this woman would become a part of their investigation.

Anya's friends had arrived. Better late than never thought Shona. Her idea of first thing and their idea seemed to differ. She let them off given the fact that they'd probably had a late nigh. They worked in bars like Anya.

They did simultaneous interviews with Shona, Nina and Abigail taking the lead.

"Interview with ..." She gave the rest of the spiel.

"How long have you known Anya Peirs?"

"Since we were at the same school. We have been friends long time."

"Why did she come to Scotland?"

The woman's gaze darted around the room as though looking for an escape hatch. Definitely avoiding the question thought Shona.

"An answer today would be good. We're looking for a murderer here."

The woman's shifty eyes filled with tears but Shona was unrepentant.

"Why did she come to Scotland?"

The witness decided it would be in her best interests to answer. She looked down at the table and mumbled, "To marry Bertram."

The way she was acting it was obvious that the marriage had been one to get Anya permission to live here.

"Why did the rest of you come over here?"

There was the gaze again.

"I take it for the same reason."

"Yes. But we love our husbands."

I bet you do. "I'm not interested in anything you did to get here. I'm interested in a murder. What was Anya's relationship like with her husband?"

"It was good. Bertram is very kind man. Looked after Anya well."

"Did she have any friends other than the women who are in here today."

"No. No one. We come together and are friends

together." The slight movement of her eye's said she was making this up.

"I find that difficult to believe. She must have had some other friends."

"No other friends."

No matter how many different ways Shona tried to cajole her into giving the right answer the woman would not be budged.

"That lot are hiding something," said Nina, when they pooled findings.

"I agree, but we can't exactly arrest them for something we think they might know," said Shona.

"I even said we'd deport them all if she didn't tell me what she was hiding," said Nina. "Still nothing."

"We can't deport them. They're legally married with nothing to say they're up to something dodgy," said Shona.

"I know, but it was worth a try."

They'd have to dig around a bit more. There was more to Anya than met the eye.

Trisha Leyland's parents looked to be in their eighties. Shona was feverishly trying to work out the age difference when the woman put the record straight. It turned out they were her grandparents.

"Tricia's mother died of a drug overdose when she was three. We brought her up. Have you found her?" This last was said in a voice devoid of all hope.

"I'm sorry to have to tell you that we have reason to believe that Trisha is dead."

The woman's shoulders sagged. Tears ran down her cheeks.

The man just looked bewildered. "Where's my tea?"

"You'll get it in a minute love." Despite her grief

the woman's voice was gentle. She patted his hand.

"I need to wet my whistle. When is my tea coming?"

A dead granddaughter and a husband with dementia. Some people's loads are almost too heavy to bear, thought Shona. Despite this she still had to ask the woman some questions.

"When did you last see Trisha?"

"About four months ago. It's unusual for her to go off. She knows what we went through with her mother, and she's a good Lassie."

The woman's use of the present tense was a good indication that the news hadn't yet properly sunk in.

"Did she tell you where she was going that day?"

"Aye. She went to spend the day with a pal. Jesse, said she never turned up."

"Is Jesse a male or a female?"

"A laddie. I think they were more than friends but she never said."

"Did Trisha know an Anya Peirs or Daisy Murray?"

"I think she went to School with someone called Daisy. I'm not sure though. It was a long time ago and my memory isn't what it used to be."

"What school did they go to?"

"St John's on Harefield Road."

"Do you know Jesse's address?"

She scribbled down all the details they needed and handed over the piece of paper.

"Thank you. You've been very helpful. I really am very sorry for your loss. I can assure you we will be doing everything to find your granddaughters killer."

"I'm confident that neither of them are a killer," said Shona as they climbed into the car.

"With her arthritis she'd have difficulty cutting up steak, never mind a dead body," agreed Nina.

A side trip to St John's elicited the information that both Trisha and Daisy attended the School at the same time. Whilst it gave them a link, no one on the present staff remembered them. So they still didn't know if they were good friends or even friends at all.

Time was wearing on and Shona was exhausted. She could have curled up on Fagin's bed and slept for a week. Unfortunately, rather than knocking off early she had to interview four men who had dated Anya. They'd been pulled from their place of work and were not happy.

"My boss is threatening to sack me. I said I didn't have time and you lot handcuffed me."

"You should have asked your boss for time off and come with us nicely."

"I've not got time for this."

"And I've not got time to stand here arguing with you. If you'd shut up and let us ask some questions we might all get home before midnight."

The man shut up.

"Are you a member of meetyoursouldating.com?"

"What's it to you? I don't have to answer that."

"Yes you flaming well do, otherwise I'll be charging you with perverting the course of justice." Shona had moved her upper body forward. She'd had enough of this jumped up pompous windbag. "Now answer the question."

"Yes. So what."

"Did you date a…" she looked at the documents for dramatic effect. She knew the name off by heart. "…Daisy Murray?"

"I think she was one of them. I've dated hundreds of women." He leaned back in his chair and crossed one short stumpy leg over the other.

I bet you have, thought Shona. Once only. "How many of them end up dead?"

That wiped the smug look of his face. He was now sitting bolt upright. "Dead. What do you mean dead?"

"I'm sure a hotshot accountant such as you knows what that means. Now that you've got a grasp of the depth of the trouble you're in maybe you'll answer my questions. Did you know Daisy Murray?"

"Yes. I dated her once. She didn't want to go out again. Not that I cared, she was weird."

"What do you mean weird?"

"She looked bored, as though she was going through the motions."

Why does that not surprise me, thought Shona.

"When did you date her?"

"About four months ago."

That would fit with the timescale her mother gave.

"Did she say anything about anyone bothering her? Tell you anything about herself?"

"She barely said a thing. She wasn't the usual type of woman I go out with. She didn't want to know anything about me."

Shona thought maybe she didn't have to ask anything about him. He probably talked about himself non-stop.

By the end of four interviews they were no further forwards. The other men said she didn't seem interested either.

"Jason, why did you think she might have been in to women?"

"meetyoursouldating.com has a huge area for the LGBT community to meet. The area for male female dating is smaller."

"It just goes to show you shouldn't make assumptions."

28

His mind had moved him on. The question of how to kill someone couldn't be answered until one knew the human body intimately. His research also moved on. Books on human anatomy joined his growing research pile. He devoured every single organ a human body contained. Diagrams were committed to memory. He could recall them instantly. He thought about nothing else. His parents provided him with a skeleton after he gave them some guff about wanting to be a doctor. They didn't care as long as he was quiet. He could recite every single bone, strip the skeleton and put it back together again - blindfold.

From the skeleton he added knowledge of the joints to his brain. Muscle and ligaments followed. Then he memorised where every organ was in the body, what it did and what would happen if it stopped working. All sixty thousand miles of human blood vessels were committed to memory. He could recite at will where every nerve went in the body and what it controlled. Lastly, the skin was added, layer by precious layer until it was full thickness. A perfect human body which he could picture at will.

This knowledge did not exist only in his brain. He excelled at science at school. This made him popular as he was always willing to help others in his class.

"Gol, be a sport and help me with the functions of the liver."

Gol, short for Goliath, his height giving him the

nickname, was happy to oblige.

Women fell at his feet when he could tell them exactly what he was doing to them, where his fingers were travelling.

But much more important than acclamation and fame, this knowledge would allow him to move forward with the important research. How does one kill another human and how does one dispose of them? This question had still not been answered.

29

Before Shona had a chance to interview Ally Cauldwell she was dragged along to another crime scene. She'd been summonsed by one of the uniform who were currently guarding her flats.

"I don't need any Coppers escorting me to my crime scene."

"That may be the case, Ma'am, but we're not employed by you. We've been told to follow you there and that's what we are going to do." He didn't seem fazed by Shona's attitude. He had been told to protect her and nothing was going to stop him doing his detail.

He did follow her, all the way to Clatto Park on the other side of Dundee. It wasn't raining, but the weak early morning sun was doing it's best so send light through the tree canopy.

Yet again, at first light, Shona found herself looking at a partially covered body part. This time it was another arm, or at least a hand with a couple of fingers missing.

"It looks like we've found the arm thon finger belonged to," said Peter.

"Oh good. We'll be able to reunite them." Lack of sleep and hidden fear gave a sharp edge to Shona's tone. "The fingers might have been carted off by an animal."

"There are no' many wolves in Scotland. There's some talk of reintroducing them though."

"Stop wittering on about animals, Peter. Who was out in the woods at this obscene hour to trip over our arm."

"Two laddies from the University Officer Training Corps. They were getting ready to go out on exercise so were sleeping in the woods overnight. They thought they heard something strange so got up to investigate."

"I don't think whatever they heard would uncover that. It looks like it's been there a wee while."

"He was having a pee when he noticed it," said Roy, who had joined them.

"Don't tell me someone's been urinating on my crime scene."

"Fraid so, Ma'am. They weren't exactly worrying about your crime scene up until then."

"They're quite bright so moved away from the area and called us. They're with the rangers and having a cup of tea as we speak," added Peter.

"From your in depth knowledge I'd say you've already interviewed them."

"Roy did. I just asked them a few questions."

The others had joined them and eventually Iain arrived.

"Good of you to come. Have you been having a wee lay in?"

"I've been here for about an hour, Ma'am, taking photos. But there's something strange going on." He hesitated.

"Well, are you going to share it with the rest of us, or keep it to yourself."

"It looks like there's been a wild animal in the woods. There are some very strange prints." He indicated she should follow him. She, and the others, did. He stopped in a muddy clearing and pointed to some animal prints.

"What do you mean it looks like a wild animal?" Shona's face indicated she was decidedly underwhelmed. "This is Dundee. The nearest you get to a wild animal is Camperdown zoo. Even then most of them aren't that wild."

"Ma'am, I'm telling you. That's like no print I've ever come across."

"Do a cast and work it out. Seriously, you'd think I'd be able to get through a case without the weird and wonderful creeping in."

Iain leapt to it and started mixing the materials. The others were looking on. Nina was trying her hardest not to laugh. Probably the best move as Shona wasn't in the mood for high jinks.

"Take that smirk off your face, Nina. You lot can start a search. If you happen to find Bigfoot's footprint be sure to let Iain and me know."

At that Nina lost it. The others were also sniggering. They hurried off before Shona could lambast them.

Shona waited whilst he took photos and compared them on his phone. Eventually he said, "It looks like the footprints belonged to a bear."

"A bear? Unless Camperdown zoo have been walking their bears around the countryside it's impossible."

"You never know, Ma'am," said Peter. "They're a strange lot up at that zoo."

"Even they are not that strange. Could someone have broken the bears out and taken them for a walk?"

"I don't think so. Have you seen the bear enclosure? It's fairly well guarded."

"Nina, come with me. We're off to talk to the zookeepers. Peter, you're in charge. Keep this lot occupied. Mary will be here soon and will allocate tasks."

As Shona walked off she could hear Peter say, "Come on you shiftless lot. Move yourselves and put some wellie intae your jobs. You're looking like a bunch o' wasters."

Shona grinned. Peter could always be relied on to keep the juniors moving. The thought cheered her right up.

Although the wildlife centre wasn't open the staff were in and about their duties. Shona managed to attract someone's attention. A wave of her ID card and she was inside the park.

"You don't happen to be missing a bear do you?"

The man looked at her as though she'd gone doolally tap.

"How the frig would we be missing a bear? They're locked up tighter than the crown jewels."

"Signs indicate that one of them has been wandering around Clatto Park."

"Impossible. Come with me."

He showed her the locking systems and security measures on the bear enclosure. He was right. Edinburgh Castle would have been easier to get in to. The bears were all present and correct.

"Is Goldilocks coming soon," said Nina.

"Ha flaming ha. We haven't heard that one before, have we?"

"Could one of the keepers have taken the bears out?" asked Shona.

"Those bears don't leave that enclosure. Even if they're ill the vet sees to them in there."

Shona remembered the missing fingers and said, "Are your wolves all accounted for as well?"

"What? Are you a bunch of jokers? All our animals are safe and well and in their enclosures. There's not a breech in the place. You can look around if you want."

"No need to get snippy, said Shona. "I'm doing my job and that means I can ask you any question I feel is necessary."

"Sorry. Honestly we run a tight ship here. The animals are well looked after, well fed and kept safe and secure."

"I believe you. Thanks for your help."

Just to be sure the pair of them took a walk around the perimeter of the zoo. He was right. Well maintained and locked up tight.

Mary had the team hard at it when they returned. She looked up as they approached. "Well I never, it's the ringmaster herself. Roll up, roll up, all shapes and sizes of animals in here."

"Have you been thinking that up since you got here?"

"Pretty much. We're taking our time in the hope we find the fingers. We're waiting for the dogs to turn up."

"Do you think the finger at the flat could belong to this hand?"

"It's looking likely. The fingers appear the same shape and length. We'll need DNA to confirm. Do you think there's any significance in their cutting off two fingers?"

"Confirmation our killer is fruitloop material. Other than that who knows. Probably just a clever ruse to have us running all over the place."

"I get the feeling this is going to be all we'll get at this site. I'm so far behind with autopsies I'm going to have to double stack them in the drawers. I've called other pathologists in to help with the routine stuff."

A voice whispered in Shona's ear. "I see you're at it again."

Despite the fact she'd had a falling out with Douglas, the sound sent shivers from her head to her toes. She whirled round. "Douglas. I feel like I haven't seen you for ages."

His smile melted her heart. "It's only been a few days but I know what you mean. I've been knee deep in School stuff. Trust me you're better off out of it."

"I take it you're here for an update and not just to provide me with the low down on your life."

"I am that."

She told him what was going on. "Bears? You did say bears?"

"I most certainly did. If you're free you can escort me back to the station. It seems I need a bodyguard to go from A to B."

Back at the Gulag's Shona had a prisoner waiting for her. Ally Cauldwell had been provided with bed and board overnight. His general demeanour said he didn't appreciate it. A skinny little runt, with pockmarked skin and a black patch over one eye, he didn't appear to have much going for him.

"Why have you bas—"

"Shut it Mr Cauldwell. I'm not in the mood."

"I've—"

"I said Shut up. I've not got time for you to be roaring about police oppression. You know fine well what you've done and it's illegal."

"Nobody told me what I'd done. I was handcuffed and dragged in here. I'm telling yi it's police brutality."

Shona got one of the policemen to fetch Jason.

"DC Roberts, did you read Ally here his rights."

"Yes, Ma'am."

"Did you inform him what he was being arrested for?"

"Of course, Ma'am."

Shona turned back to Ally. "Listen here you little weasel. Answer my questions and make it quick. If you don't you wont be able to eat for the foreseeable future." She'd kept her voice too low for the recording.

She'd also made sure her mouth couldn't be seen by the cameras.

"You're threatening me."

"No I'm not. Did anyone hear me threaten Mr Cauldwell."

"No, Ma'am." There was a chorus of agreement from Jason and the uniforms.

Shona shoved the photo across the table. "Why were you wandering around Dundee with a crossbow."

"There's nae law against carrying a crossbow."

"There is when it's fully loaded and out in the open in the middle of the city square. I'd say that comes under threat to kill."

Ally went white.

"What exactly were you going to be doing with the weapon?"

"I was taking it to a man down the pub."

"With the bolt in, ready to fire. Even you can't be that stupid."

"I want my lawyer."

"With pleasure. You're going to need one when you go in front of the Sheriff anyway."

With Ally safely tucked up in his cell Shona grabbed Peter, Abigail and Roy.

"I need you lot to go and search Ally Bally's place. It shouldn't take you long as it's at the bottom of the hill, above a shop." The bottom of the hill was what the locals called the bottom of the Hilltown. Shona had learnt something in her time here.

"I think it's the flat above Big Brenda's shop," said Peter looking at the address.

"Interesting. Off you go now. Call in to the Sheriff's court and I'll have a warrant waiting for you."

"Oh, before you go, Peter, what's with Ally's pirate impression?"

"Lost his eye in a pub fight. He was at the wrong end of a knife. He refuses to use a prosthetic, says he looks better with the patch."

"Someone ought to tell him otherwise."

The team came back like conquering hero's bearing the spoils of war. Instead of shields and golden goblets they carried a crossbow and a number of bolts.

"Looks like he's our boy," said Peter.

"I'd like to think so, but something doesn't sit quite right. Take the crossbow into evidence. I'll get forensic tests done to see if it could have fired the bolt that killed Angel."

The Gods' were obviously smiling down on Shona, as neither Runcie nor McCluskey were representing Ally. His lawyer was a casually dressed young woman who appeared to be about fifteen. She shook Shona's hand.

"Marion Selkirk. I've heard a lot about you."

"Is this your first case by any chance," asked Shona.

"Yes, how did you know?"

"Just a wild guess. I'll give you some time with your client." Shona felt like she was throwing the girl to the wolves. By the time they had finished the interview Shona was reassessing her opinion of the girl's abilities. She was sharp as a tack and ten times as deadly.

"We've found a crossbow in your flat Mr Cauldwell, along with several bolts to go with it."

"It is not an offence for my client to have a crossbow in his possession. He is not under the age of eighteen."

"I appreciate that Miss Selkirk. However, if I suspect that your client has, or is going to commit an offence with said crossbow, then I have the right to arrest and detain him."

"Which offence is my client supposed to have committed?"

"There's a corpse in the mortuary which has a crossbow in its back. Your client has a crossbow. Add both together and it equals murder."

"You have no evidence that my client was involved in this murder."

"No, but I do have his crossbow and we will be looking at it very carefully. If it matches then your client is going to be spending a lot of time at Her Majesty's Pleasure."

"I never murdered anybody. You cannae say that."

"Ally, I'm going to be crawling all over this. While I'm doing it you'd better think very carefully about giving up whoever you are protecting."

Once they were out of the room Shona asked the lawyer if she would like a drink.

"Better not. If I'm seen to be consorting with the police my client might not be too happy." Marion smiled.

"I can't believe they gave you this for your first case."

"I was top of my class. Aced everything. They must think I'm capable."

"Good for you. I'm sure I'll be seeing you again before too long."

Shona took one of the bolts down to Mary. She wanted her to have a quick shufty before everything went off to forensics.

"Is this the same as the one in the back of your corpse?"

"Looks pretty much like it. I would say it's twenty inch."

"The crossbow and bolts have been sent off to forensics. They'll give us a definitive. Another question. Could someone with one eye use a crossbow with any degree of accuracy?"

Mary thought for a minute. "It wouldn't be impossible, but definitely difficult. Someone would have to be an expert and well practiced."

"Thanks, Mary. I'll have to buy you a drink when this is all over."

"I'll have died of exhaustion before then."

Yet again Shona was waiting for forensics to provide her with results. She paced around her tiny office as though that would make the results magically appear. She knew, deep down inside, that Angel's death was linked to the Alexeyev's or Petrescu. Maybe both. Unfortunately without putting pressure on their only witness it would be difficult to prove. Luckily the DNA lab was working overtime to get results to her. She now had a definitive on the Torso. It belonged to Daisy Murray. Not that this helped her in any way, but it did give the relatives more of a body to bury. Her fingers drummed a tattoo on the table whilst she thought about the case. She realised she was tapping out Scotland the Brave. She must be returning to her Scottish roots. Thinking of all things Scottish she suddenly remembered something and dashed through to the squad room.

"Peter, did we ever do the interviews at the castle?"

"We did, Ma'am. Nothing to report. The staff have all worked there for about sixty years and are loyal to the core. The current laird and his wife are in their dotage and can hardly walk never mind murder anyone."

"Have they any offspring?"

"One daughter who lives in Australia. She's been there for donkey's years. Visits about every couple of years."

"Thank goodness it's come to nothing then. I'd hate to think we'd missed anything. Knowing my luck the killer would be lurking there and I'd be rotting in jail for the rest of my natural."

"Relax, Ma'am. Your safe."

The chief was on the warpath. Not that Shona was surprised. This was his normal state.

"Why was I not told that there had been a development in this case?"

"A development. I don't know what you mean, Sir."

"Was there, or was there not, another body part found this morning?"

"Yes, Sir. However, I didn't realise you wanted to be appraised every time we found one."

"Don't be impertinent Inspector."

"I'm not trying to be impertinent, Sir. I didn't want to waste your time."

"I've had the chief constable on the phone wanting an update and I had no clue what he was talking about."

"Sorry, Sir. I will update you immediately if anything else occurs. We do have one interesting problem. It looks like there were bears wandering around our crime scene."

"Bears. You did say bears?"

"I did, Sir. Camperdown Zoo say they aren't missing any, so we have no clue what is going on."

"I despair of you Shona. How I landed up with you heading up my CID team I will never know."

You interviewed me thought Shona. She was also thinking that it would be a great idea to chuck the chief into the bear's enclosure and let them have fun.

The sound of a ringing phone, coming from her office, interrupted her reverie.

30

Whilst plotting the perfect kill he still had to function as a normal human being. This normality provided a bright cloak for his dark, murderous intent.

He was popular with both men and women. The life and soul of the party, he was invited to every one of them. Everyone wanted to be his friend. The parties gave him rich fodder for his thoughts. It would be easy to kill here. Something slipped in a drink and then he would leave. No one any the wiser. Many hours were spent thinking through the nuances of this. He came to the conclusion it was too risky. Someone would mention he had been there and the cops would come knocking.

Still this information, this research, was crucial. Knowing what wouldn't work brought him one step closer to knowing what would. Not one minute of his time was wasted.

31

Shona bolted back to her office and grabbed the ringing phone. It was the desk sergeant.

"I've got a Mr Henry St. John-Smith down here. He said he needs to speak to you about his missing wife."

"Is that the lawyer?"

There was a muffled conversation at the end of the line and then the desk sergeant said, "Aye. It is."

"Bring him up."

The team were stunned. Particularly Nina. "Can I be in the interview?" she asked.

"Definitely not. You're the last person who should be in there. Peter, you're with me. We need someone experienced."

Before they went to the interview room she pulled Peter into her office.

"Is there anything I should know about Henry? Any insider info?" Peter was the fount of all knowledge when it came to Dundee and its inhabitants.

"Nothing untoward or dodgy. He's a nice bloke, a good lawyer and most people like him."

"I was hoping you'd say he'd been married six times and all his wives disappeared under mysterious circumstances."

Henry looked like he'd lost thruppence and found tuppence. Haggard didn't begin to describe him.

"Would you like a cup of coffee or tea?" Shona thought holding on to something might still his shaking

153

hands."

"Coffee with milk and two sugars."

Despite a slight tremble Henry's voice was stronger than Shona would have imagined. Still he was a lawyer and used to talking, she thought. It probably came naturally to him.

A passing copper was dispatched to bring drinks. When he returned they started the interview.

"Mr St. John-Smith—" She stopped. "— Can I call you Henry? Your surname's a bit of a mouthful."

"Please do." Even in grief he was polite."

"Henry, can you tell us what happened?"

"I haven't seen my wife for three days. She went out to look for some maternity clothes. She didn't return."

"Is your wife pregnant? I thought you were separated."

"Yes to both questions. We got back together when she got pregnant. We were heading that way anyway."

Thank goodness that Nina isn't here, thought Shona. She'd have thrown a hairy fit at that point. Usually sunny natured, Nina was a terror when something riled her.

"That wasn't the impression we got when you were dating my Sergeant."

"I wasn't really dating her. I was still in love with my wife. Anyway we only went out once and I told her I was married."

"I still think it's a bit strange for someone who loved their wife so much."

"What are you going to do to find my wife? You'd be better discussing that than my love life."

The hard edge to Henry's voice was unusual for the usually beguiling lawyer. Shona was willing to put it down to grief. She kept her voice soft so as not to be accused of antagonising him. He might be a grief stricken husband but he was still a lawyer.

"What have you done already?"

"The usual stuff - phoned her friends, rang the hospitals, spoke to her family. I even rang the hospitals in Edinburgh, Glasgow and Aberdeen."

"Do you not think that's a bit far flung for someone who was only popping out to Mothercare?"

"I was clutching at straws. I was desperate. The hormones were making her do strange things."

"Do you think she could have walked out on you again?"

"No. She was looking forward to having a family. We were secure about our future together."

"Why did you separate in the first place?"

"You don't need to know that."

"I think you'll find I do. If your wife, and unborn baby, are missing then every single thing about your life is my business."

"I say you don't. It isn't pertinent."

Okay, play it your way, thought Shona. I'll be digging up the dirt on both of you before you can get home."

"I will need you to go through every single thing your wife does in her life - clubs, friends, groups, social media accounts. In fact, the works. Sgt Johnston will take it all down."

"I'm not giving you permission to go through her social media accounts. That's too personal." Tears ran down his face.

"Your a lawyer. You must know we don't need permission. We'll get a warrant if needs be."

"Why are you being so intrusive?"

"Why are you trying to block us? Have you got something to hide?"

A hint of a smile broke through the tears.

"I know. I'm sorry. I'm just trying to protect my

wife."

"We can only protect her if we find her. We can only do that if we find out everything about her."

"I can't bear the thought of anyone rifling through her life. It seems clinical somehow. As though I'm betraying her."

"We'll be sensitive."

She left him with Peter to sort out the finer details.

"Roy, work your magic on the Interweb. I need all you've got on Lucinda St John-Smith and her husband Henry."

"Henry St John-Smith? The lawyer?"

"The one and only."

"I can't go too far on investigating him. He'll have it thrown out of court."

"I'm off to get a warrant so we'll be able to do anything that's legal. Keep it legal this time though. Neither of us want to be visiting the cells for anything other than professional reasons."

She moved over to Nina's desk. "Nina, Abigail. I want you both on standby. The minute we get the names of Lucinda and Henry's mates. We'll be visiting a few."

"We'll need someone else."

"You're right. Hoy, Soldier Boy. You're on standby as well."

"For what, I wasn't listening?"

"You pair get him up to speed. I'd better let the boss know what's going on."

The chief was not impressed with anything she said. "You had better treat this with kid gloves."

"Of course, Sir. But I do need to investigate in case a crime has been committed."

"Shona, he's a lawyer. He could chew us up and then swallow us, in court."

"I appreciate—"

"He's also in the local lodge with George Brown, so they are very good friends."

"I knew Pa Broon would be in the middle of this before long."

"That's enough Shona. Treat Ex Lord Provost Brown with respect. You will not upset him."

"Yes, Sir." She wondered if she could take out a contract on both the chief and George Brown. She'd happily pay more than the going rate.

"You'd better undertake a wide search. Show her photo around everywhere. I'll get uniform drafted in to help.

"Thank you, Sir. I appreciate it."

32

Shona and Nina knocked on the blue front door of a huge house in Clearwater Park. This was a new housing development on the outskirts of Dundee.

"These houses must cost a bomb," said Shona.

"I don't think you'd get much change out of a million squids," said Nina.

"How the other half live."

The door was opened by a woman who was still in her dressing gown. They could hear a baby screaming in the background.

"Whatever you're selling I'm not interested."

Judicious placement of a foot stopped the door from closing. Shona said, "Mrs Ferguson I'm DI Shona McKenzie. Can we have a word?"

"Why? What's happened? Is it Glen?"

"No. It's not bad news. We need to speak to you about Lucinda St. John-Smith."

The woman ushered them in. She picked up the squalling baby. She shoved her left breast in its mouth and peace descended.

"Is Lucinda still missing?"

"Yes. Her husband is concerned."

"Is he now?"

"From your tone of voice can I take it that you don't approve of him?"

"He was always cheating on Lucinda."

"Is that why they split up?"

"Yes, she said she didn't want anything more to do with him. Mind you it took her long enough."

"How long have they been married?"

"Eight years. She left her first husband for him."

What a convoluted relationship, thought Shona.

"What was their relationship like when they got back together?"

"She seemed happy. Happier than I've seen her in a long time. It might have been the fact she was pregnant."

"Do you know if her husband was ever violent towards her?"

"I'm not sure. We didn't see each other often. She did call off a few coffee meeting saying she was ill but I never thought anything of it."

"Where did they meet?"

"I think at a club but I couldn't be a hundred percent sure. I just remember she was full of the joys gabbling on about the amazing man she'd met. She was in love from the get go. Walked out on Frank pretty much straight away."

"Frank was her first husband? Do you have his address?"

"Sorry, we lost touch with him after that."

When they left the house Shona said, "Next stop the registry office. Let's find out a bit more about Frank and pay him a visit."

The registry office trip elicited the information that she had been married to Frank Zabic.

"We're awash in foreign surnames in this case," said Shona. "What I wouldn't give for a few Mcs or Macs. It's not that I mind the foreign surnames I just can't get my tongue around them."

"Where's it from," asked Nina.

"How the flaming heck do I know. Do I look like a dictionary of surnames?"

"I was just asking."

"You don't half ask some stupid questions sometimes."

Nina laughed. "You can always count on me."

Shona joined in the laughter. "It's a good job we're friends."

Arriving in Arbroath and knocking at Mr Zabic's front door, his accent indicated he was from Glasgow. His crew cut and heavily tattooed torso indicated he might be a thug. After they showed ID he ushered them in."

His brows furrowed, he said, "What do you need me for, Inspector?"

"We would like to ask you a few questions about your ex wife, Lucinda. When did you last see her?"

He went rigid. His fists clenched. Shona was ready for action and wished she'd brought at least a stun gun.

"Not since the day she walked out the door. I wanted nothing to do with her after that."

My, my, thought Shona. Eight years hasn't taken the edge off then?

"Why are you asking me about Lucinda? I would have thought you'd be interviewing the maniac she married?"

"Why do you say he's a maniac?"

"Anyone who snatches someone's wife from out under their nose is a maniac. Even if they're a jumped up poof of a solicitor."

"Do you know anything else about him?"

"Apart from the fact I would like to rearrange his features with my fists, then no."

"Mr Zabic, issuing threats in front of the police does not bode well for your future."

"Why are you asking about Lucinda anyway? What's she done?"

"Her husband has reported Lucinda missing."

"If that sick bastard has done anything to Lucinda

I'll string him up by his balls."

"Mr Zabic. That is enough. One more threat or swear word out of your mouth and I will arrest you. Is that clear?"

"Do you expect me to just stand by when that tosser might have done something to her?"

"That's exactly what I expect you to do? Now, when you were married to Lucinda did she ever do anything strange?"

"Never, we did everything together?"

Not quite everything mister, thought Shona. She went for a night out and left you in a heartbeat. She was hardened to the average human's ability to delude his or himself.

"Did she ever go away for a few days, just for time to herself."

"No. I'm telling you everything was normal till that—"

"If you both went away for a few days was there anywhere in particular she liked to go?" Shona cut another possible tirade off at the pass.

"Yes. The Isle of Skye."

"Any particular hotel."

"McKinnon's Highland Hotel. Five star luxury all the way for Lucinda."

"Thank you Mr Zabic. We'll be in touch if we need anything else."

When they were safely back in the car Shona said, "If Henry was dead then Zabic would be my number one suspect."

Nina shuddered. "What a horrible little man. No wonder Lucinda left him. At least Henry can hold a conversation without issuing threats."

33

On returning to the station Shona rang the hotel. There were no single women staying there at the moment. In fact no women of Lucinda's age at all. So another dead end.

"Abigail, get on to A&E up at Ninewells. See if Lucinda had a history there. Also any other A&E departments within a fifty mile radius. Lucinda might have been moving around to avoid abuse being detected. Tell them we've got a warrant. I'll get one and give you the number."

As Abigail picked up the phone Shona said, "What did you get from the visits you made?"

"Nothing much. It seems like they had the usual squabbles. Henry couldn't keep it in his pants so that's why she left him."

"I thought Mr Charismatic was a bit too good to be true," said Shona.

"What I can't understand is why she would go back to him if he was like that," asked Nina.

"Pregnancy does weird things to your hormones. She was probably nesting." She paused and then added, "Henry did seem genuinely happy they'd made up. Looks like he got a shock when she upped and left."

"Serves him right. You'd think he'd treat his wife right after that."

It took some time for Abigail to ring round all seventeen of the hospitals.

"How can there be so many A&E departments in

one wee area?" she asked.

"This is not a discussion on NHS Scotland for Pete's sake. What did you find?"

"She'd been to Ninewells a couple of times. Once for a broken arm and once for bruising round her kidney."

"So it could be abuse?"

"She said she tripped down the stair and broke her arm. Her slipping and bouncing of a fence when she was running explained the kidney."

"They both seem plausible but you never know."

She strode across to Roy's desk and slapped a piece of paper down.

"One warrant. Do your damndest on the net search."

Roy, glanced up and then his fingers continued their dance on the keyboard. He didn't utter a sound. Roy and computers were a match made in heaven.

Before she'd returned to her office her mobile phone rang. It was the desk sergeant.

"Jock's here to see you. I'm sending him up."

"Take him to interview room one."

Shona sent someone to fetch some grub from the canteen. She told them to bring it in about ten minutes. They always made sure that Jock left the station well fed.

Fagin jumped up as she entered the interview room. He started yelping and nipping at her hands. She ruffled his fur before hollering out of the door, "Jason, come and take the mutt to get some food."

Jason came at her bidding and Fagin was carted off to visit Doreen in the canteen. Shona was certain a couple of sausages had his name on them.

"Nice to see you Jock. How can I help you?"

"It's how I can help you. Well I think it'll help you. I found this in a bin behind the supermarket." He pulled a little box from his pocket. Shona took it and opened the lid.

34

The way to kill someone was slowly fermenting in his mind. A rough plan was taking shape. It still needed some development but at last he felt that he just might be able to do this. However, there were more stages to his extensive research. Nothing could be left out. Attention to detail would allow him to carry out the perfect murder. It also meant he would get away with it. A warm glow coursed through his body at the thought. Sex could not have been more pleasuarable.

The woman walked along the road with not a care in the world. Her long hair, the colour of burnished copper swung with each step. She held her large handbag close. You couldn't be too careful. There were pickpockets about. She stopped to look in shop windows, and entered one. She exited carrying a paper carrier displaying a designer name. She was lost in the middle of a surging Saturday afternoon throng. In the bustling streets no one paid her much heed. Or so she thought.

The man followed her at a safe distance. He knew everything about the woman. He had studied her over several months. He now knew her so well that his heart almost beat in time with hers. His pace matched hers as they walked along the high street. In a few minutes she would enter the hairdresser. He would watch from the cafe across the road. He knew she would leave in exactly thirty-three minutes. A creature of habit this one. Didn't she know it was safer to mix it up? Change your movements. She was a target waiting for a killer. He mixed things up. He never watched from the same spot twice. Never wore the same clothes. H changed hats, coats, trousers, and shoes. No one would remember him.

A few minutes before she was due to leave he paid his bill. The minute she put one foot on the pavement he looked at his watch, folded his newspaper and stood up. The case was on once more.

Despite all this meticulous observation she would live. He was not ready yet. At this point it was only research. This woman did not know how lucky she was that she would not be his first.

35

Nestling inside the box was a finger. It smelt worse than Jock if that were possible. Shona had thought that now he was indoors he might have made more liberal use of toiletries. They'd supplied him with enough when they set up his flat.

"Jock you should have called us and we would have come. You've removed evidence from a crime scene."

His face fell. "Sorry, lassie. I should have thought. I wanted to keep it safe for you."

"I know Jock. No use fretting. Let's get it in to evidence."

Once it was safely registered and deposited she returned to Jock. He was tucking in to a huge plate of steaming stew, with plentiful helpings of mashed potatoes and vegetables. The smell made Shona's stomach rumble. "What were you doing in the bins? Now that you're inside you must get benefits."

"It's no' much and I wanted to make sure Fagin was fed."

"We'll get some dog food to you, and something to fill up your cupboards as well. Don't go hungry Jock. You know where the free grub is. Visit any church and they'll help you."

"I don't like to bother people Shona."

"Jock, you're no bother."

She went to find Jason. "Take Jock home." She handed him fifty pounds from her purse. "Get him some dog food and human food on the way there." She pulled out another note. "And buy him twenty quids worth of toiletries. It might encourage him in their use."

"You're not as hard as you seem, Ma'am."

"Tell anyone that and you'll find out just how hard I can be. You might be missing body parts as well."

"My body parts are not the right sex for your case, Ma'am."

"Jason! That's quite enough. Remember I'm your boss."

"Sorry." His face said he wasn't in the slightest sorry. He did make a mental note to be a bit more circumspect in the future.

Jock having been sorted out and, hopefully, sweetened up, Shona decided to call the lab who were doing the DNA results. She was keen to know the owner of the finger.

"Ma'am, much as we'd love to help you we're not God. Miracles are not in our remit."

"I'm sure you'll understand I'm anxious."

"I've got people on this full time. You'll have the results soon. You have my word on that."

"Thanks ..." She thought for a few seconds and then, "What's your name."

"Kelly."

"Kelly, I think you might just be my favourite man in the whole wide world."

She could almost feel his blush over the phone.

She had no sooner put it down than the phone rang again. The voice made her come over all peculiar. "I'm blessedly kid free as I've foisted them off on their long suffering gran. Fancy going for a drink?"

"You know, I think I do. Where and when?"

She put the phone down, released the troops from the salt mines, and went off humming cheerily. Despite severed limbs, life was good. It was very good indeed

36

The way Shona felt in the morning there was nothing for it but a fry up and a run to work. She was over the limit anyway. It wasn't a good look for a cop to break the drink driving laws. They were particularly strict on this in Scotland. Zero limit and zero tolerance. Not that she would ever do it anyway. She'd seen enough fatalities from drink driving in her time in the police. She didn't want to be one of them.

Coffee wasn't going to cover it this morning. She downed three glasses of water and felt a bit more human. She thought slugging back Talisker on a school night wasn't the healthiest way to live her life.

"I dinnae think I've seen you look at a glass of water before." Peter had arrived. He needed a cup of the road tar he usually referred to as tea.

"Don't ask. We'll just say the procurator fiscal is a bad influence."

Her hangover was forgotten when the phone rang.

"I've got that DNA result. The finger belongs to one Anya Peirs."

"Kelly, You're the man of my dreams."

"Glad to hear it."

Another piece of the jigsaw completed. This got her day off to a fighting start. She cheered up considerably more at the next bit of news.

"Ally Cauldwell wants to speak to you, Ma'am," said Roy. "We've sent for his lawyer."

"I hope he's ready to sing like the proverbial

canary."

It turned out he was ready to sing like a whole flock of canaries. He'd obviously decided he wasn't going down for murder.

"It wasn't me that killed Angel."

"You've already said that. So what's new?"

"I was just holding on to the crossbow for somebody."

"I'm dying of boredom here Ally. Give me something I can work with or I'm charging you with murder."

"Deek Forbes did it."

"Who's he?" Shona looked at Peter who shrugged.

"He's one o' Bogdan Petrescu's hit men."

Shona sat bolt upright in her chair. Ally shrank back. "Give me more."

"What more do you want?"

"Did Petrescu order the hit?"

"Yeh. Yeh he did. He was sending a message to the Russians. I'm no' really sure about that bit, though."

"Are you telling me Angel worked for the Alexeyev's."

"Aye, the absolutes."

"The absolutes?" Shona was puzzled.

"Vodka. Absolute Vodka." He looked at her as though she were 5mls short of a dram.

What is it with Dundonians and nicknames thought Shona?

"Where will we find Deek Forbes?"

"At Joey's."

"It's ten o'clock in the morning," said Peter. "You know fine well it'll no' be open. Where's his gaff?"

"The multi's at the bottom o' the hill." Shona, despite her Oxford upbringing had learned that these were tower blocks of flats. Her Scottish language was coming along in leaps and bounds.

"You'd better be telling us the truth." Shona leaned forward and said, "If you're not I'm letting both Petrescu and the Alexeyev's have at you."

"Why are you threatening my client? Being in the police you'll be aware that it's against several laws."

"Relax. I'm only having a bit of fun. I'm sure both lots are able to find him without my help."

Peter hauled him off kicking and screaming. He hurled him into a cell and said, "Shut up. I've a headache already and you're making it worse."

"At least one murder's solved. Or nearly solved. Lets' go get our gangsters."

Before they went she asked Iain to check the crossbow for prints. "I want to know about every person who's gone within a mile radius of that weapon."

You'll have it. No need to worry.

Arresting Petrescu involved a warrant, a lot of shouting and swearing, several guns and a bit of a fight. By the end of it they had Petrescu in the cells along with several of his henchmen. A bullet had winged Jason so he and Roy were currently up in A&E.

"I seriously need to think about replacing him," said Shona. "He spends more time in A&E than on the job."

"What will we do with that lot?" asked Nina.

"Leave them to cool their jets until we've got Deek in custody as well. There will be plenty of time to process them all then."

"But—"

"We're wasting time, lets go."

Arresting Deek Forbes was almost, but not quite, as exciting. He was wielding a crossbow. He'd obviously replenished supplies since his original one was taken into custody. He let off one bolt which

missed them by a mile and then Peter and Abigail
pounced on him. Abigail applied some ancient Chinese
trick that had him on his knees begging for mercy. He
was soon handcuffed and dragged out to the car.

"There's never a dull minute around here is there,
Ma'am?" said Abigail. She was grinning ear to ear. "It
wasn't as lively as this on Skye."

"I'm wondering if I can get a transfer there."

Deek was swearing up hill and down dale that he was
innocent. He wanted his lawyer who turned out to be
the battleship herself.

"Mrs McCluskey, how lovely to see you," said
Shona. "I was just saying that I wondered when we'd
see you again."

Margaret McLuskey didn't know how to take this.
She was used to Shona's scathing tongue. Her eyes
narrowed and her lips grew thinner. I didn't realise that
was even possible thought Shona, mesmerised.

"Your client is waiting, and of course is protesting
his innocence."

"That will be because he is innocent."

"Your ability to delude yourself never ceases to
amaze me, Margaret."

"You can call me Mrs McCluskey."

"Your lucky I'm not calling you Vanguard."

"What? Why are you being so rude?"

"Never mind. Toddle off and speak to your client."

With pursed lips and full sails billowing the
battleship steamed off. Shona had no doubt she would
be in for a roasting from the chief later. It was worth it
to have a bit of sport with McCkuskey.

"Ma'am, you've brightened this place up no end.
Its been fun and games since the minute you turned
up," said Peter.

Nina and Abigail were holding their sides they

were laughing so hard.

"You pair. Get a grip. Peter you take Nina to interview Petrescu. Abigail you're with me. Deek might spill if he thinks you're going to torture him again."

"I didn't torture him, just applied a tiny bit of pressure in the right place."

"You've got to teach me that trick."

"My client states he is innocent and I believe him. This is a gross miscarriage of justice."

"The judicial process hasn't completed yet so there's not a miscarriage of anything never mind justice. Could you be quiet for a minute and let me get on with the interview."

McCluskey threw her a look that could have frozen hell but her mouth stopped making a noise. Shona threw up a silent prayer of thanks.

"Mr Forbes. I have a witness who states that this weapon is yours."

Deek took one glance and said, "Never seen it in my life before."

Shona shoved the picture closer. "Take a better look and consider your answer. Are you sure it's not yours."

"Are you deaf. I said no."

"I take it you were thinking about some facial realignment," she said in a low voice. "I will gladly help you out."

"What are you talking about? You're no' making any sense."

"Speak to me like that again and you'll be changing the way you look."

"You can't threaten my client."

"I'm not threatening him, I'm saying he'll be feeling, and looking a wee bit upset."

She passed over another sheet of paper. "This says

that your fingerprints are all over the weapon in that photo. Now does it belong to you?"

Deek licked his lips and his eyes darted towards his lawyer.

Shona's hand crashed down on the table. Deek leapt up.

"Sit down and answer the damn question."

"It might have done. I don't know."

"Your fingerprints were also found on a crossbow bolt we recovered from a victim."

She'd popped along to see Iain on the way there. He'd cross matched Deek's fingerprints to the one on the weapons and bingo.

"Derek Anthony Forbes, you are under arrest for the Murder of Mr Gabriel LaShawn. You do not have to say anything, but it may harm your defense if you do not mention, when questioned, something which you later rely on in court."

"I didnae do it. I've been framed." He looked at his lawyer. "Tell them."

For once in her life the battleship had nothing to say.

She was right about the ticking off from the chief. She barely had to time to make a pot of coffee before she was hauled in front of him.

"I've had Margaret McCluskey in here saying you were rude to her and threatened her client."

"It's not true on either point, Sir. I remained within the law."

"Did you remain professional?"

"That point might be somewhat debatable. I did my best."

"Inspector, I have no clue what to do with you."

"Perhaps let me get on with my job."

"You might be cheeky to the rest of Dundee, but

you will not talk to me like that."

"Sorry, Sir."

"I've also had Pa..."

Shona's lips twitched but she held back the smile. I'm in enough trouble she thought.

"I mean Ex Lord Provost George Brown on the Phone. McCluskey is his God Daughter and he's not happy that you are not allowing her to do her job."

"I gave her all the time in the world to do her job. It's not my fault the old battle axe is useless."

The chief couldn't contain his smile. "I appreciate that Runcie and McCluskey could be considered as bad as their clients. However, that does not give you carte blanche to treat them badly. That will be all."

Shona left his office wondering how she could get training in how to use a crossbow. The chief would look much better with a crossbow arrow through his heart. Saying that he had been fairly pleasant this time. Maybe, just this once, she was being a bit mean.

Her elation at having solved a murder and locked up some gangsters didn't last long. Although she'd arrested Petrescu, she'd merely cut off the head of the snake. Somehow or other it would grow back. Also she'd knocked out the Alexeyev's main competitor giving them freedom to rule the city once more. Sometimes justice could be a double edged sword. There was also the little matter of several dead women to be investigated.

The team were hard at work when she went into the office. Doing what she wasn't sure as they were somewhat stalled.

"Peter, can you go and chuck Ally out on to the street. Tell him not to go anywhere. He's our star witness. Don't tell him that though or he'll disappear into the wilderness."

"I'll sort it out. Nae need to worry."

Shona had no doubts that he would. Peter knew more about policing Dundee, than she could ever hope to know.

"Ye'll need to ring Angel's parents tae tell them their wee bairn's murder's been solved."

"What? I think I got the gist of that but spell it out in English just in case."

"You'll need to let Gabriel's parents know their son's murderer has been found."

"Don't you think I know that? It's next on my list."

"Well you never know Ma'am. I like to keep you on the straight and narrow."

"Go give Ally the old heave ho. You can stop telling me about my shortcomings as a police officer."

A chat with Gabriel's parents did not go well. Shona could almost hear the wailing about the phone, despite the fact they were in America.

"What are you doing to find my boy's killer?"

Shona wonder if they were quite right in the head.

"Did you hear what I said? His killer is in the cells. So he's not free to kill another day."

"It took you long enough. The police in the states would have done this much more quickly."

"I'm sure that's true however we did it as quickly as Scottish law would allow."

"You'll be hearing from my lawyer."

"I shall look forward to that. If there's anything you need to know please contact us immediately. I'm happy to discuss everything with you."

What a pigging nightmare thought Shona. As if I haven't got enough trouble with Dundonian lawyers, now I'm worrying about American ones.

"If that woman thinks I'll be phoning her every

two minutes she's got another think coming," said Shona to Peter, who had joined her.

"What are you talking about? Sometimes I think you're talking in riddles."

"Me talk in riddles. That's steep. Half the time I don't know what you're talking about at all."

37

The investigation had stalled somewhat. Well not so much stalled as flatlined. Shona was wondering how she was going to be able to resuscitate it. She didn't have one thought as to where to go next. Going into the main office she navigated her way to Roy's desk.

"Where have you got to with the search on our man Henry."

"Not much on Henry. However, I've been searching his dead wife's social media accounts."

"Don't keep me in suspense. Was there anything we should know about?"

"The usual stuff that women talk about on these sites. A few interesting things though."

"Spit it out, I haven't got all day. It's not that I'm running an investigation anything. For heaven's sake Roy, more women could be dying while you are carrying on like this."

"It's like you said, they did seem to argue a lot. People don't seem to realise when you moan about your husband online it's not private."

"All wasn't sweetness and light then?"

"Nope. Quite the opposite in fact. He was abusive towards her. Not fisticuffs, but they did seem to do a lot of shouting."

"You can't arrest a man for murder on the grounds that he had the odd tiff with his wife. Plus it's one side of the story."

Roy did not look happy. "You're right," he said. "Get a printout of anything she said online. I want them on my desk soonest."

"I've also done some digging on Anya's social media. Not much in there. Most of it's in Polish."

"Have you had it translated?"

"Google translate gave me a bit of an idea. had to work out some things though. Mostly a perfect life with her husband. Madly in love blah, blah blah."

"Unremarkable. Why are you telling me this?"

"Private messages say he used to knock her about."

"Good catch. Print them out and get them translated properly."

The clicking of the keyboard could be heard as Roy turned to his task." You've got it Ma'am. It'll be with you yesterday."

"Nina, come to my office I need to speak to you now."

The aroma of freshly brewed coffee filled Shona's small office as they took their seats. They took a few minutes to devour a couple of huge cream cakes before starting.

"What was Henry like when you were dating him," asked Shona.

"What do you mean?"

"Did he ever give you any indication that he could have a temper?"

"Not really. He was a bit shifty when he told me about his wife. You'd expect that though."

"He didn't try to control you in anyway?"

"We only went out once. He didn't have time to try anything on. To be honest he was more interested in talking about how much he loved Lucinda. Made me want to throw up."

"Nina, I need you to think. It's important."

Nina's brows furrowed and silence descended. They both sipped and savoured their coffee.

Eventually Nina said, "He was a bit sharp with a

couple of people who came up to talk us. I just thought he didn't want to share me with anyone else."

"You didn't think that was a bit strange?"

"I suppose now that you mention it, it was. At the time I just thought it was him being a lawyer. They don't like people interfering."

"Do you think he displayed the potential to be overprotective and controlling?"

"It might've started to annoy me if we'd gone out any longer. It just seemed endearing on a first date."

" We'll have to arrange for Henry to come back in. Can you sort it please, but I don't want you in the interview."

"You'd maybe get more out of him if I was in interview."

"I'm sure you're right, but I'd like to keep the heavy guns until later in the game. I'll pull you out of the wings if things get tricky."

Nina left. Shona swallowed down the last dregs of her coffee before picking up the phone. It was answered within a couple of rings.

"Yes." Henry's voice was terse.

"It's DI McKenzie here. Would you be able to come and talk to us? I'd just like to ask you a few more questions."

"I've told you everything I know."

"I appreciate that, but as a lawyer, you know that we have to go over everything with a fine tooth comb. We wouldn't be able to live with ourselves if we left anything out."

"It's inconvenient."

"Your wife is missing. Surely you can drop everything and come rushing if we need help. Unless you're not worried of course."

"Of course I'm worried. I'm going off my head here. What are you insinuating?"

"I'm not insinuating anything. Now could you please come in and see us?"

"I'll be there in about an hour."

"I'll see you then," but Shona I was listening to the dialling tone.

"Has he been taking lessons from the chief?" said Shona to the empty room.

Henry was indeed there within an hour.

"What took you so long?" asked Shona.

"I need to have a shower and a shave before I arrived." Henry did look like he had spent time getting himself ready.

"You think your wife's discovery would be more important than grooming yourself to within an inch of your life." said Shona.

"My coming here scruffy isn't going to find her any more quickly."

"Yes, but you are arriving in a timely manner might. As you well know every second counts in a missing persons case. If you came straight here we could've started this discussion forty minutes ago. Anyway I have got time for this discussion. Some new information has come to light."

"What new information? What have you found?" Henry was shuffling around in his chair as though there were scorpions under him.

"We've been through your wife's social media accounts."

"I told you you couldn't do that. Why have you got against my wishes?"

"And I told you that we would be getting a warrant that said we could. This piece of paper has the full force of the law behind it." She shoved the paper across the table for Henry to appraise." As a lawyer you will appreciate it is our job to look into every single facet of your wife's life."

"What did you find there?"

"What do you think we found there?"

"I'm sure I don't know."

"You're really beginning to annoy me. Why don't you try answering the questions and be polite and civil. Your wife could be dead for all you know and all you're doing is mucking us around. We're all on the same side here so let's work together."

"I'm not trying to avoid your questions. I'm not on social media. I have no clue what my wife does on there."

"According to her you have more than a few problems in your marriage."

"So we argued. Everyone does and everybody sounds off about it to their friends. It just so happens we live in a digital age."

"So, what did you argue about?"

"This and that. How am I meant to remember? My wife's missing, and all you can rattle on about is why we argued."

"You're a lawyer for Pete's sake. You should know why it's important. Your wife was telling all and sundry online that you were trying to control her. Is that true?"

"Of course it's not true. Why would I try to control her?"

"You tell me. She was saying you wouldn't allow her to do anything. Every time she wanted to go out with friends you'd find an excuse to stop her."

"What a load of rubbish." Henry's voice was so loud it would've cracked the lamp if Shona hadn't shushed him. "How dare you say this. Are you trying to frame me? Are you trying to rile me? It's not going to work."

Shona shot the papers across the table. Some fell on the floor. Henry picked them up and glanced at them. His face went so red she felt that it would not end well.

"What have you got to say about this?"

"What do you want me to say? It's a pack of lies. I can't believe she'd say things like this about me. She could ruin my reputation."

"Your wife's missing Henry. Surely her safe return is more important than your reputation."

"I love my wife. So I have no idea why she would say this about me. I've done nothing to warrant it."

"Perhaps your having multiple affairs may have something to do with it."

"That's not true. Who's feeding you all these lies?"

"Most of her friends are saying it. We seem to be getting the same story from every last one of them."

"They're all against me."

"For goodness sake. Why would a bunch of housewives collude against you? They've better things to do with their time like look after their husbands and families. So let's just say it's true."

"This is preposterous. They didn't like me because she left her wastrel first husband for me."

Shona couldn't fault Henry's assessment of Frank.

"Give me a break Henry. I haven't got time for this. Start telling the truth or I'll think you have something to hide."

"It was a bit rocky. But we sorted it out. You know that. You're the one wasting time asking me stupid questions instead of finding my missing wife."

"They are not stupid. I'm trying to find out if your wife may have left you again. Now, were you, or were you not, having affairs while you were married? Is this why your wife left you in first place?"

"Yes. I had a couple of affairs. Two. Not multiple They were in the past. I've told you time and time again that we had reconciled. We were excited about the baby. No, more than excited, my wife was ecstatic."

"And what about you? Were you ecstatic? We haven't heard much about your feelings on the matter."

"I couldn't have been happier. I've always wanted to be a father. We even know the sex of the baby. It's a boy." His eyes filled with tears.

"We would like to search your house. Are you happy for us to do that?"

He nodded and put his face in his hands.

"So you are saying yes we can search at your house? For the benefit of the recording you don't want us to get a warrant?"

He looked up misery etched in every line of his face. "No. No, you don't need a warrant. I'm happy for you to go in to my house and look for anything you want. I've done nothing.There's nothing I need to hide."

"I would like you to wait here while we do the search. You can use one of the spare offices in which to work. I don't want to inconvenience you even more."

Before she could leave the interview room, Peter entered and beckoned that she come out. He closed the door carefully, and whispered something in her ear. She promptly told Henry he was free to go but not home.

"We will have officers posted at the front and back doors of your house. As a lawyer you will appreciate why we are doing this."

She turned and walked out of the door of the interview room.

38

Yet again Shona found herself trailing out to a cold, wet crime scene. This time it was in Pitlochry. Given the lateness of the hour it was also as black as Satan himself. The local POLSA had secured the scene, but it appeared as though he had done so by the light of a few ineffectual torches. This would have been somewhat difficult, given that yet again dripping trees surrounded them. What I wouldn't give for a crime scene that's in a lovely, clean, dry, warm house, thought Shona.

"Are there lights on the way?" asked Shona.

"There should be, but we're having trouble with the roads around here. There's been a lot of flooding."

"Where are they coming from and what is the expected arrival time?"

"Aberdeen. ETA any time they get here."

"How am I meant to carry out an investigation, when I can't see three inches in front of my nose?"

"You may want to start by interviewing Tam over there." He indicated an old man and an even older collie dog both of whom were shivering under a tree. "He was the one that found the body."

"Body! You mean a whole body?" The POLSA looked at her as though she what a fingerprint short of an investigation.

"Of course I mean a whole body. That's what I said isn't it?"

"It's just that we seem to have been a bit short of entire bodies recently. It's been more a case of bits and pieces than one glorious whole."

"I don't mean to be rude, Ma'am, but why are you

185

investigating this anyway? It's a bit far from Dundee."

"You're right it is a bit far from Dundee. However, the powers that be have decided I'm the woman for the job. Much as I'd love to be tucking into a carryout with my feet up on the sofa, I'm here. We'll both have to make the most of it."

"I'm not complaining, Ma'am. You have a good reputation round here."

"That's a lot of confidence you're placing in me."

She decided to take pity on the shivering pensioner. "Is there anywhere around that I can take Tam. He looks like he needs somewhere warm."

"The nearest you'll get to warm around here, is my van. You can switch the engine on." He handed her a set of keys.

Shona installed the pensioner in the front seat of the van. She switched on the heating and also the overhead lights. Lights were a bit of a misnomer, given the feeble beam that appeared. Still they were better than the inky darkness outside the window.

"Tam, can you tell me your surname please?"

"Banister." Tam was a man of few words like many elderly Scotsmen.

"I know it must be difficult for you, could you please tell me what you saw?"

"It was Bailey what found her." He indicated the elderly Collie in the backseat.

"She was barking at something. My daughter gave me a new fangled phone and it's got some sort of light on it. I shone it to where the dog was to stop the confounded noise. That's when I saw it."

"What did you see Mr Bannister?"

"The woman. She was all sprawled there."

"Did you touch her or anything else?"

"No I didnae."

"Did you check to see if she was alive?"

"There was no need for that. One look and I knew she was dead."

"What made you so sure?"

"You'll see for yourself Lassie. Ye don't need to be a brain surgeon to work out she was long gone."

"What were you doing in the woods?"

"Taking the dog for a walk. We go there all the time."

"Do you take the same route every time?"

"Every single time. The dog's a creature of habit. She'll not go anywhere else."

"So the body wasn't there yesterday?"

"No it wasn't. Bailey would have found her then if it had been."

"That will be all. Thank you very much for your help Mr Banister. Stay here in the warm and one of my officers will be here to take your statement shortly."

The lights took a couple of hours to arrive. In the meantime, they did what they could by torchlight. This meant sticking to the perimeter as they didn't want to ruin the main crime scene itself. Shona was wet, miserable and cold through to her bones.

"I'm thinking of applying for a job in Tesco's. At least it's inside."

"You'd be bored by break time," said Peter.

"I'm bored here waiting for the lights to arrive. I might as well be bored warm."

"You're always telling us off for moaning," said Nina. "How come you get to do it?"

"It's one of the perks of being the boss."

Iain interrupted to the cosy chat. "Ma'am, you're not going to like this."

"Spit it out. I haven't got time for soft soap."

"You know what I was saying about Bigfoot. Well, it really does look like Bigfoot's print this time."

"I hope you're joking. Even if you are, it's not funny."

"I'm as serious as the plague, Ma'am. Someone with big feet and no shoes has been wandering around here."

"In this weather? It's like the arctic tundra out here. They'd have frostbite in a few minutes."

"I'm taking a cast." Iain finished the conversation by grabbing a bag of the powder needed to make the cast.

Shaking her head Shona wandered over to Peter. "Bears and Bigfoot. All we need are a couple of anaconda's and a troupe of dancing horses and we could start a travelling circus."

"I've no clue what your on about, Ma'am," said Abigail. "I could have sworn you said Bigfoot."

"I did. Iain has just informed me that Bigfoot has been strolling around my crime scene."

Abigail couldn't talk for laughing. After a few minutes she managed to gasp, "I thought the Chinese were bad for believing in myths and legends."

Shona couldn't help but join in. "It's not funny. How am I meant to tell the chief this?"

"Rather you than me. We didn't have these strange goings on in Skye. It was pretty straightforward there."

"Are you thinking of returning?"

"No way. I wouldn't miss this for the world. It's the best job ever."

"I wish I thought that. I'm thinking of going back to Oxford. My job there was a piece of cake compared to this."

"No way. You'd miss us too much to do that." Roy joined in.

"Sometimes, with you in the mix, I'm not so sure."

Roy just grinned. He and Shona had come a long way. Just a few months ago he'd have helped her pack up her office and led the cheerleading team. Thankfully the lights arrived and they were able to approach the dead woman. Shona, went first treading carefully, and fully suited up. The wood was large and the body placed deep within it. Although placed did not to do it justice. It looked like someone in a tearing rush had chucked it. One glance and Shona knew exactly what their witness meant. It was indeed a whole body. However, that fact could be debated. The head was completely severed from the rest of the body. It had also been battered to a pulp. It was about 2 feet away. Shona stopped and surveyed this scene. She allowed Iain to take copious amounts of photos. The woman was naked apart from a pair of stockings held up by a suspender belt.

"I'd say this is part of our investigation, but I'm not entirely sure. It might be the missing Lucinda but she doesn't look very pregnant. Hardly likely to need maternity clothes as yet."

"I'm not sure we can say that, Ma'am. From the way someone's laid into that head it could belong to anyone."

"I suppose your right. We could have found two pieces of the jigsaw in one place."

"I was never very fond of jigsaws as a child," said Abigail. "Now I've gone off them for life."

"I don't think I'll be able to face them in quite the same way again either," said Shona.

Someone, who lacked the ability to make a sensible decision, had called the local police surgeon to pronounce the victim dead.

"What did you drag me out here for? Anyone with half a brain could tell you that this woman is dead."

"Nothing to do with me or my team," said Shona. "You might want to look more locally for your culprit.

He hurried off grumbling to himself. There's a man

who loves his work, thought Shona. I don't know what he's complaining about. He'll be getting paid extra to come out and do this. I, on the other hand, get zilch. There wasn't much they could do here, that the local force couldn't pick up. The local pathologist agreed that they could send the body to Dundee.

"I heard Mary was having a difficult time of it at the moment."

"We're all having a difficult time of it," said Shona. "We're doing a good line in filling the mortuary freezers with various body parts."

"I take it you're Shona Mackenzie. I've heard all about you."

"I bet you have. You and the rest of Scotland."

She moved over to the team and told them they were dismissed. It was now 10 PM and they'd had a long day. They weren't going to have a lot of time for sleep this night.

By the time Shona got home she could only muster up the energy to feed a yowling Shakespeare. She then fell into bed fully dressed and was snoring fit to bust the ceiling, within seconds.

39

He finally decided that the best way to dispose of a body was to cut it up in the first place. It could then be distributed around the countryside. Burying it in different areas meant that he would be less likely to be caught. Body parts were unlikely to surface all at the same time. He weighed up the advantages and disadvantages of his plan. He knew he would have to be meticulous in his approach. There was no room for error when it came to leaving his DNA. He would also have to avoid detection when disposing of the body. Careful research and planning should help him to get around this.

He still hadn't worked out how to kill them in the first place but the first part of his plan was in place. In theory that is. The practice would need to wait. He would develop an intricate game of human jigsaw. Should the police ever find any of the body parts, they wouldn't have the others. A feeling of great satisfaction came over him. Knowing that he'd pinned down one tiny part of this plan was more exciting than sex, and that was saying something.

The next part of his research involved him reading books on pathology. The librarians now thought he wanted to be a pathologist or a surgeon. He could legitimately read books on how to remove diseased or injured limbs. He devoured books on autopsies and managed to blag his way to a work placement in the mortuary. Nobody was allowed anywhere near a dead body but he could soak up the atmosphere revelling in the fact that he was close to the action.

However, he still wasn't anywhere near knowing the practicalities of what it felt like to cut off a limb. He needed to know the pressure required and the exact blades which would need to be used. This needed more thorough research, but he was in no doubt as to how he would achieve it. That was the next part of his research. His plan, his life's work, would soon come to fruition. He was willing to wait and savour the anticipation.

He was happy in the knowledge that he had finally answered the question how does one dispose of a body. He felt his plan was fool proof.

40

Shona bounced out of bed full of the joys the next morning. She switched on the tassimo and let the coffee brew whilst she showered and dressed. She was taking the first divine caffeine fuelled sip when the Phone rang. For once it was nothing to do with dead bodies. In fact it was Douglas. "Where were you last night? I rang several times and you didn't get back to me. I was worried. You mustn't go off somewhere without telling me."

"Douglas, I'm trying to do a job. What makes you think I'm going to stop it and phone you every time something happens?"

"You had a finger posted through your door. You don't think that might give me cause for concern."

"I know you're worried, Douglas, but that doesn't mean that you can wrap me up in cotton wool. I'm fine."

"Promise me you'll take care."

"I promise. But only if you promise me to stop fussing."

"It's a deal."

The saltmines beckoned so she had a quick shower, filled a travel mug with coffee, and flew out the door. She realised that she'd left a house search swinging in the wind. It wouldn't be long before Mr Charismatic was putting in a complaint about her. The chief wasn't very happy with her right now so she better do things by the book.

Her first task on arriving at the office, after putting on a pot of coffee, was to ring the sheriff. As always Sheriff Struthers was happy to oblige.

"You do like to upset the fine upstanding citizens of Dundee, Shona. I didn't issue this many warrants in a year before you arrived. Now I seem to be sending them over to you every week. Send someone along the warrant's yours."

Whilst she was waiting for it to arrive, She went to update the chief. He was incredulous.

"Did I hear you say Bigfoot?"

"You did, Sir."

"Bears and now Bigfoot. Are you trying to give me another heart-attack?"

"Not at all, Sir. I agree it is strange. The killer is obviously playing a game with us."

"Well find out what the game is and get it stopped. Now. Do I make myself clear?"

"I will do my very best, Sir."

"Make sure you do. I need this sorted. How am I meant to update the chief inspector with tales of wildlife and Bigfoot. I've had quite enough of this and you McKenzie."

Shona left his office wondering if she could maybe entice Bigfoot along to the chiefs office. This thought made her grin. By the time she returned to the main office Roy was waving the warrant. They were good to go.

"Roy, you stay behind and see what you can find on Bigfoot sightings in the United Kingdom."

"You mean I'm being left behind, Ma'am?"

"My your quick, Roy. You got it in one."

Henry and Lucinda lived in a ginormous old house up the top of the Perth Road. There was obviously no shortage of money in being a solicitor. However, the vast garden was overgrown and the house looked a little unkempt.

"Looks like he spent most of his time womanising, rather than keeping the house up," said Peter.

"I'd say you're right."

Henry had given them a key so they let themselves in.

"Our Lucinda wasn't exactly houseproud either," said Shona. "It stinks in here."

"You're telling me. It looks like a few bombs have exploded around the place. It's going to take us hours to process this," said Jason.

"You'd better hurry up and get your gear on then. Fully suited and booted. Hop to it."

They hurried to do her bidding. Every one of them had been at the end of one of Shona's tongue lashings. They were not in a hurry for a repeat. With white coveralls, the blue shoe covers and a protective glasses, they looked like Martians. Going through the flat was painstaking work. Every single surface had to be dusted for fingerprints. Then came the slow process of checking the whole area for blood. The only place they found evidence of blood, was in the bathroom. That was in small amounts and could have resulted following an accident with a razor. Mouldy dishes sat piled up in the kitchen sink.

"Jeez. You think a lawyer and his wife we be able to do a bit of tidying up," said Iain.

"Do you think we can take his computers?" asked Nina.

"The warrant doesn't cover that, so no."

They scoured the garage and shed with the same meticulous attention to detail. Still nothing to be found.

"I was hoping we might find an axe, a chopper or a boning knife," said Shona.

"It looks like our lawyer is as clean as the

proverbial whistle," said Peter. "All we've managed to get is sore feet and I'm starving."

"All you ever worry about is your stomach. Concentrate on something else for a change." Shona felt the same but she wasn't going to say so.

The first thing they did on returning to the station was head to the canteen. Having not had anything to eat since the previous lunchtime Shona was in the mood for a full cooked with all the trimmings. Doreen, who thought Shona rocked, was happy to oblige and even bunged on an extra couple of sausages for good measure.

"Doreen if you ever need anything come straight to me. It's yours whatever it is."

"Och, Shona, I'm happy to do it. Somebody has to look after you. Anyway I know your granny and she'd be after me if I didn't see your right."

They say the army matches on its stomach. This was also true for the police. At least it was true for Dundee CID. She had to muster up enough energy to tell Henry St. John- Smith that he was free to return home.

Shona thought she might have a bit of breathing space, but it was not to be.

41

He was right. His plan was foolporoof. Apart from the CCTV cameras that is. Dundee, like every city in Scotland, was riddled with them. His research informed him that there were more camera's in most Scottish cities than in San Francisco, Sidney or Paris. He needed to know the position of every single one of them. This led to a long, laborious search on foot and by car. This later moved online as technology advanced. He kept a meticulous map that he updated regularly.

He left nothing to chance, changing the days, times and months of his search. He did normal things whilst he was about it. Popped into the library, the pub, the supermarket or the local store. Just one man, amongst many, carrying out his routine tasks.

In many ways this was the single most important part of his plan. Once he had plotted where they were, he could then plan how he could avoid them.

42

The translation of Anya's Facebook account had come back. It turned out Roy and Google translate were right. Bertram Peirs had been roughing up his wife. Or so she said. This was still allegedly rather than actual fact. Before she had a chance to call him in for interview the phone rang. Daisy Murray's mother was in reception. She wanted to talk to Shona. Apparently no one else would do.

She and Nina interviewed the woman. "How can I help you Mrs Murray?"

"I've remembered something. You asked about her boyfriends?"

"Yes that's right. I asked if she had any boyfriends and you said she didn't."

"Well she might have done."

Shona's heart beat faster. "What makes you say that?"

The woman hesitated, then, "She did say one time she had a foreign boyfriend. Funny name for a man though?"

"Can you remember what it was?"

"Andra? Arnie? Something like that."

A bomb exploded in Shona's head.

"It wasn't Anya was it?"

"That's it. I would have thought that was a woman's name. He was foreign though. They're a funny lot foreigners. You don't think it was him do you?"

"Thanks Mrs Murray. You've been really helpful."

Once they were outside the door and the woman

had left, Shona said, "Bigotry is alive and well and living in Dundee."

"Shona, that wasn't bigotry. She'd feel the same about someone who came from Fife. Anyone who isn't from Dundee is a foreigner to the likes of her," said Nina.

"God spare me. Seriously how did I end up here?"

"You love it. It's a right laugh here."

"Do I look like I'm laughing?" However she did have to crack a smile. No one could fail to be in a good mood around Nina.

"Let's go visit Bertram. We've a few questions he needs to answer."

Fortunately Bertram Peirs was at home.

"You lot again? What do you want now? I like coming to tell me you've found Anya's killer."

"Not as yet but I'm sure we're getting close. We would just like to ask you a few questions."

"How many questions do you have to ask me? I'm sick to death of answering questions. There can't be anything else you've got left to ask." He slowly folded his arms and stared at Shona.

"That's obviously not the case or we wouldn't be here." Shona's tone was sharp.

"So what do you want to ask? I'm fed up of all of this. I don't have time to keep entertaining you lot."

"I would hardly call it entertaining," said Shona. "You are aware we're investigating your wife's murder aren't you."

"Do you think I could forget? It's imprinted on my brain. How could anyone ever do this to Anya?"

It took long enough for him to turn on the grief, thought Shona.

"Was your wife seeing anyone else behind your back?"

"What do you mean? Of course she wasn't. Anya and I were in love. She would never do that."

"We have reason to believe that she was."

"No. Absolutely not." He was quiet, and then, "Who is saying such things? When I find out who it is I'll kill him. How dare he say things like that about Anya."

"I've told you before not to issue threats to the police. Will you rough them up like you did your wife?"

"I didn't hit my wife."

"We have reason to believe you did."

"That's not true."

Shona changed tack trying to shock him into giving something away.

"Was your wife having a lesbian affair?"

Bertram bolted to his feet and shouted, "You can't go around saying things like that. Anya only had eyes for me. She wasn't into women."

"Did she ever mention anyone called Daisy Murray?"

"No. No she didn't. Is this who she was meant to be having this mythical affair with?" He didn't even pause to think.

"We're not sure."

"I want to talk to this woman."

"You'll have difficulty, she's dead as well."

Bertram sank down on his chair. He didn't seem to have anything else to say. It was as though all the stuffing had gone out of him.

"You might see now how much trouble you may be in."

"Why? Why am I in trouble?"

"Because it looks like to me that you found out about this affair and bumped them both off."

"I'm not saying another word to you lot without my

lawyer present."

"Fine! Come with us you can phone your lawyer from the station."

The good news was that the battleship McClusky was not Bertram's lawyer. The bad news was her brother, Angus Runcie, was. Shona thought it was too good to be true that she would manage to get through a day without seeing either one of them. Surely there must be more lawyers than them here in Dundee. Saying that every low life in the city had one of them as his or her lawyer so the law of averages said that they would be here more often than she would want.

"Why have you arrested my client? You have no evidence that he's committed any offence."

"I was merely asking him a few questions about his wife. You know the one that was murdered? Then he decided he wanted a lawyer so we had to ask him to come in here."

"Well you'd better make it quick. He doesn't want to be here any longer then he needs to be."

"Do you think we want your client to be here at all? Why are we even having this discussion? I've an interview to conduct."

Shona stomped off and Runcie scurried to catch up.

"Now that we are comfy in an interview room perhaps you might want to answer some of our questions. Has your memory returned yet."

"You can't talk to him like that."

"Like what? I haven't said anything yet. If you'd shut up we might be able to get on with it and we can all go home soon."

The lawyer did as she requested but the murderous look in his eyes told Shona that she was for the high jump later.

Shona handed over daisy Murray's photograph.

"Have you ever seen this woman before?"

Both Bertram and his lawyer studied the picture carefully. After a few seconds Bertram said, "No definitely not."

"Are you absolutely certain."

"A hundred percent certain. The only friends my wife ever had were the ones who came with her from Romania. They were stunners. I'd remember someone this plain."

Shona had a sudden urge to rearrange the man's features. How Anya had ended up married to someone this odious Shona would never know.

"Mr Peirs we would like you to stay here while we search your house."

"My client does not agree to that."

"It doesn't matter what your client agrees to. We have a warrant that says we can search his house any time we want."

"Why what has he done?"

"That's what we are trying to find out. If he hasn't done anything he has nothing to worry about. We will even establish his guilt or his innocence."

Bertram and his lawyer exchanged looks.

Shona said, "You can wait here. Would you like a cup of tea or coffee?"

She arranged the beverage and left a lawyer and his client to it.

"I can't believe we're doing two searches in one day," said Peter.

"Me neither. At least this house is a bit better than the last one we were in. I'd say either Bertram or his wife have a touch of OCD. It's a miracle we found that hair."

They repeated the search with much the same result. The place was awash with fingerprints and they would have to match them against every friend the occupants had ever had. Iain looked particularly cheerful about the fact. He was never happier than when he had a forensic challenge. All it did for Shona was make her heart sink. This was going to take forever and she didn't have forever to solve this case.

"Have we got any specimens of Daisy's fingerprints?" asked Shona.

"I've got her brush back at the lab. I should be able to get some nice prints from that."

"Iain you are a legend."

"Why thank you kindly, Ma'am."

Back at the station Iain got to work. Shona, in the meantime, needed to have a word with Roy. As was usual his head was down and his fingers were flying over a computer keyboard.

"What's the skinny on Bigfoot then Roy."

"Easy peasy. You can buy shoes online that simulate animals or Bigfoot. That's where our unusual prints come in."

"So the killer's toying with us?"

"It looks like that."

"This is all just one big game to him. He doesn't care that he's playing with human lives."

"I'd say that's what makes him dangerous, ma'am."

"Dangerous? He's freaking nuts. There can't be any other explanation from this."

Roy turned back to the keyboard.

"What are you working so hard on?"

"I'm still delving deep to see what I can come up with on Henry or Bertram."

"Good luck with that."

Shona informed the chief that the little matter of the bear and Bigfoot had been cleared up.

"You took your time."

Perish the thought that he would ever give me one tiny atom of praise, thought Shona. She was now thinking that incarcerating the chief, the bear and Bigfoot in one room might be a jolly good idea.

43

Books were all very well but there was no substitute for hands on experience. He needed to sense what it was like. To have the tactile feeling of flesh under his hands. He needed to understand the pressure involved when a knife cut through skin. Only the sensation of holding a meat cleaver or saw in his hands and using it on muscle and bone would allow him to develop the necessary skills. He thought carefully about where he could legally do so. It was apparent he would not gain these skills practicing on humans. He therefore needed to think of a different way of gaining the experience.

His parents were surprised when he said he had a job in a butchers shop. However, they did nothing to stop him. They never did. They thought it was important for him to explore and embrace life in all its different formats. He assured them that it was merely a way to make some extra money. He was saving so it wouldn't cost them as much when he went to university. The job had come up and why not. They'd get discount on the meat as well. They would be shocked to know that it was death that occupied his mind.

The first step was to know his equipment intimately. Every knife saw and cleaver was memorised. He could handle them more slickly than the experts. Then he needed to make sure his equipment was sharpened. To know it would slice through the joint as if it had the consistency of butter. He first had to employ a meat saw. Within a few weeks he was an expert in using it in many different ways. He knew how to remove the legs from the carcass in the most efficient manner. He knew you would be able to transfer these skills to a human corpse. There was nothing difficult about it. A human was just another animal. Things were moving on. Still, he waited for the right time. In these things, as in all things, timing was everything.

44

"It's time we interviewed Anya's friends again," said Shona. "It seems to me that the information they were hiding was the fact that Anya was gay."

"Fifty quid says you're right," said Nina. The women were brought in and interviewed one at a time.

"It's come to our notice that Anya may have been gay."

The woman looked down. She didn't say a word.

"Was she gay?"

Still the woman said nothing.

"For goodness sake answer me. Your friend is dead what are you hiding?"

Still nothing.

"If you don't give me an answer right now I'm deporting you back to Romania."

"Yes. Yes, she was gay. Anya had always been a lesbian. That's why we left Romania."

"So why on earth did she get married?"

"So she could stay in the UK."

"Were the rest of you up to that as well?"

"No. We genuinely love our husbands."

"Were did you meet your husband?"

"He was on holiday in Romania. We met in a nightclub."

"I'm a bit puzzled as to where Anya came into this?"

"She wanted to get out of Romania. Her father was too strict. He would've killed her if he had found out."

"And yet she ended up dead anyway."

The woman burst into tears. Shona felt guilty. She softened her voice.

"I'm sorry. That was a bit harsh. You've been really helpful and I'm sure that will help us find her killer."

The other two women came up with the same story. it looked like Anya was running away from one situation and ended up in one that was a hundred times worse. Shona could not believe that her being gay had led to this. Not in this day and age.

"I still think Bertram has something to do with this," said Shona.

"He's squeaky clean though, Ma'am. There's nothing we can pin on him at the moment," said Peter.

"And don't you think I know that."

Ian had had the first glimmer of good news. "I've managed to get a print off Daisy's hairbrush. It matches one of those in Anya's flat."

"Good work Iain. So Daisy had definitely been there."

"Shall we get her husband in again?" said Peter.

"Not at the moment. Let's bide our time and see if Roy can come up with anything on the Internet."

Her mobile rang. "Shona Mckenzie."

"I've got an update on the DNA. Finger number two is a match for Trisha Leyland."

"Thanks Kelly. That's a kiss I owe you."

"Why are you promising to kiss a girl?" asked Peter. "Will the procurator fiscal no' be jealous?"

"I'm sure he will be but lets not worry about that at the moment. If we don't tell him then it won't bother him."

"I like the cut of your jib."

She passed on the news.

"Which one was finger number two? I'm completely lost."

"With all these limbs and digits flying around I'm

not surprised. Get everyone into the briefing room and we'll update the board and each other."

With a neatly laid out plan on the board things looked much clearer.

"The only unidentified now," said Abigail, "is the corpse from Pitlochry."

"I'm still willing to stake my pension on the fact that our unidentified will turn out to be Lucinda St. John-Smith."

"Did they know each other? Was Lucinda gay?" asked Nina.

"Unlikely given the fact she was pregnant. Unless she'd had IVF. Maybe she was bi-sexual."

"See what you can find on social media, Roy. I haven't got the energy to interview Henry again."

"Righty ho, Ma'am. I love my job. I get to spend my day on the Internet and Facebook."

"Don't get too to used to it. We could yank it away from you any minute then what would you do?"

"That's like taking a lollipop away from a wee bairn. You wouldn't do that to the poor lad," said Peter.

"Just watch me."

Roy wasn't there to listen to this exchange. He'd bounded off, full of restless energy, to do some muckraking on the world wide web.

"We haven't got much of Trisha to go on."

"I'd say the fact that she is missing a leg and one finger is a good indication of the fact that she's dead," said Abigail.

"She jolly well ought to be. We've been and gone and told her grandparents that she is."

Shona decided to have another closer look at Trisha Leyland's notes. They hadn't really looked into her boyfriend Jesse. The initial officers on the missing persons case had done a stonking job. They looked at Jesse from every angle and nothing came up. She pulled the DVD of his recorded interview, and spent an hour peering at every detail. From his general demeanour, facial expressions and his answers Shona was confident that the man had nothing to do with Trisha's death. It said in the notes that he was an accountant not an actor. No amateur could be this good. Another dead end, or so it seemed.

"Roy, add one Jesse Brown to your online searches. That's Jesse with an e not an ie."

"He's not related to Pa Broon is he?"

"Jeez. I jolly well hope he isn't. It's not in the notes so I wouldn't have thought so." Shona still sent up a fervent prayer that this wasn't the case.

"Ma'am, it's gone 19.30, Can we please go home? Everyone is exhausted," said Peter.

Shona was startled. "Of course. Sorry. This case seems to have stopped me thinking about anyone or anything apart from the dead women."

45

How to kill someone was the thought still rattling around in his brain. It was obvious one could not cut up a body until the victim was dead. This thought occupied his every waking moment. Periodically he pulled out all the books and read them again. One by one each method was dismissed. They were too complex or too difficult to access the necessary equipment. He also wanted a feeling of satisfaction from the kill. It needed to be up close. It needed to be personal. He wanted to see the look of panic in his victims' eyes as they drew their final breath.

For quite some time he thought that a paralysing agent may have been the perfect method. However, this meant holding the victim down and at the same time trying to inject the drug. He decided he might inject himself accidentally. That was not a risk he was prepared to take. He finally decided upon suffocation. It was perfect. Up close and personal and he could watch every movement his victim took. He could see the look of the fatality in their eyes as they finally realised that this was the end.

His plan was taking shape, no, his plan was nearing perfection, he thought. A virtuoso violinist couldn't have put in as much practice to achieve his goal as he had done. Every i had been dotted and every t crossed. Well not quite, but almost. There were still a few loose ends to tie up.

46

A couple of days had gone by and the case hadn't moved forward in the slightest. Shona was getting irritable and the chief was livid.

"Surely you must have some idea of where this case is going by now."

"We're doing our best, Sir."

"I have the chief constable on the phone. He wants to know why police Scotland is all over the national news. Have you seen the headlines in *The Times* today?"

"I can't say I have. I take it there's a meaty headline?"

The chief threw a copy of the newspaper at her. She took it and looked at the front page. No wonder he was riled. The headline was more than meaty, it was downright nasty.

'Scotland Held in the Grip of a Serial Killer: Police Scotland Clueless'

Whoops, thought Shona. No wonder the chief constable's knickers were in a twist. The Scottish Parliament must be asking him some difficult questions.

"What are you doing to move this forward?"

"We are following a number of lines of enquiry, Sir."

"You need to follow several more. I want this case solved quickly."

"But..."

The chief was no longer listening. Situation normal thought Shona.

The team were gathered in the briefing room. So were a number of beverages. She'd made them eat the bacon rolls in the squad room. Grease and evidence did not sit well together.

"Where did Henry come from originally? With an accent like his he's not from Dundee." She paused. "I take it from your expressions that no one knows?"

"I think it may have come up in my web searches," said Roy. "I can't quite remember where."

"Does anyone know where Bertram is from?"

More blank stares.

"If he's from around here, I'm no' sure where he got his name from. It's a bit posh for these parts."

"Roy, see if you have the information at your fingertips. If not resort to the old-fashioned method of phoning them and asking."

She had the information in minutes. Henry was from Kingston-upon-Thames. Bertram was from wick. Shona picked up the phone and dialled the number for wick police. They held no records for Bertram.

"Any scuttlebutt about him?"

"Not that I'm aware of. I can ask around the bazaars and find out for you. Give me a couple of hours."

The police in Kingston upon Thames were a bit more enlightening.

"Yes we know Henry well."

" I take it that means he had a record?"

"No. Quite the opposite in fact. He was thinking of joining the police at one point. So he did some work experience with us."

"What was he like?"

"A delightful lad. Inquisitive. He had a brilliant

brain so we convinced him he would be better off studying law than joining us."

"Did anyone have any doubts about him at all?"

"None whatsoever. He did everything we asked and did it well. From what I've heard he's a top notch lawyer now."

Shona hung up none the wiser. Another dead end. It sounded like Henry was the real deal.

The one ray of sunshine in an otherwise dreary day was that they had the DNA results for the Pitlochry corpse. It was indeed the body of Lucinda St John-Smith. Shona grabbed Peter and they went to break the news to Henry. The good news was he was at home. He did look genuinely distressed when they told him about his wife. His shoulders shook as sobs racked his body.

"Can I see her?"

"I wouldn't advise that," said Shona.

"Why? What's happened?" he jerked upright and looked at Shona. His eyes were dead.

"We'll just leave it at the fact that you wouldn't want to see her the way she is at the moment."

"I want to see her."

"I said no. As a lawyer you must understand what that means."

Henry changed tack. "What are you doing to find her killer?"

Why does everyone ask the same question Shona asked herself? That always seems to be the first one they trot out.

"The minute we have any news, you'll be the first one to hear it."

In the car on the way back Shona asked Peter, "Did he seem genuine to you?"

"Pretty much."

"He doesn't often show a lot of emotion in his

eyes."

"He's a rum one to read that's for sure.

47

Shona returned to a note on her desk. The Pitlochry coppers had been on the phone. They wanted Shona to call them back. She picked up the phone wondering what new developments could possibly have occurred. She didn't for one minute guess the revelation that her colleague was about to impart.

"You'll like this one."

"Hit me with it."

"We've witness that says it was one of your lot who dumped the body."

Shona couldn't utter a word. After a few seconds she managed to say, "One of us?"

"Our witness said that the person who dumped the body was wearing full coveralls, protectors and shoe covers."

"And he didn't think to tell us this before now?"

"He thought they were filming an episode of silent witness. He said that happened in Dundee before so could be happening again."

"I suppose he has a point. He definitely described the coveralls and everything else?"

"His exact words were, they were dressed in thon white things just like the telly. We asked a few more questions and he came up with shoe covers and specs."

The team were even more stunned than Shona if that were possible.

"Just when I think that nothing could be any stranger you pull another rabbit out of the hat," said

Nina.

"It doesn't mean its actually someone who belongs to us. Pitlochry have their own scene of crime kit," said Shona.

"Can you buy them online," asked Peter. It widnae surprise me. You can buy everything else on there."

"Good point. Roy find the answer."

He whipped out his iPhone. A few seconds later he said, "Yep. Under ten quid."

"You have got to be joking. That's probably cheaper than we pay."

"You can buy anything online these days," Said Roy.

"You're telling me?" said Shona. "It means we're no further forward though."

"So we're back to anyone could have done it." Even the sunny Nina was looking decidedly glum.

"Where do we go from here," asked Abigail.

"To the dole queue. There's nowhere else to go," said Shona. She had a feeling they were all going to lose their jobs if they didn't get a big breakthrough soon.

The gods were not smiling on her. The breakthrough would be a long time coming.

In the meantime Shona arranged to speak to the witness via Skype. Pitlochry said they would contact her when he was in the station. She wasn't sure if she would elicit anything the local force hadn't already dragged out of him. It was still worth a try.

When she started the Skype linkup she was surprised to see that the witness was about 18 years old. She thought it would be another pensioner out walking the dog. His name was Benedict Dorman.

"Thank you for agreeing to talk to me Benedict."

"It's cool."

"What time did you see this and when?" asked Shona.

"The night before it was found. About one o'clock in the morning."

"May I ask what you were doing in the woods at that time?"

"I'm a network scout. We're getting ready to go to the Brecon Beacons. I needed some night experience. I haven't been scouting as long as some of my pals."

"What exactly did you see?"

"Someone was unrolling a bit of plastic and the body fell out. I heard the thud. That's what made me look."

"What on earth made you think it was a television programme being filmed?"

"There was one light hanging from a tree. There was a camera as well on a tripod."

"What sort of camera?"

"A wee one."

"Don't you think that was strange? Television cameras are usually huge."

"I suppose. You never know these days. Everything is getting smaller."

"About what height was the person you saw?"

"I don't know. It was dark. Medium height maybe."

"Anything that would distinguish him or her?"

"They were covered from head to toe. They was more like a ghost than human. That was my other thought."

"Did you notice anything else around the area? What about a car, or a motorbike?"

He thought for a moment. "No. No I didn't. I suppose that was weird. They would have had a van if they were filming."

"Thank you benedict. That will be all."

Shona despaired of this case. She already had

bears, Bigfoot, and now a ghost. Could things get any worse?

The answer was they could get much worse. Thankfully she didn't know just how bad they were going to get.

48

There was more research to be done. It was no use carrying out the perfect crime without working out how to get rid of the evidence. The perfect crime wasn't quite so perfect if one got caught. Luckily, there were a number of books out there which could help with this. He read these hungrily, drinking up and soaking in every piece of knowledge. His brain was full to bursting with the facts and figures of cleaning agents and acids. he now knew how people used to do it and how they were caught. It was important to know what not to do before working out what was best to do.

One example, which particularly caught his attention, was that of John Haigh. He was also known as the acid bath murderer. He claimed he had murdered nine people but he was only ever convicted for six of these. His method of disposing of the bodies involved dissolving them in a bath of sulphuric acid. Despite this there was enough evidence remaining to convict Haigh. Another aspect of Haigh's case intrigued him. Haigh's claim that he drank his victim's blood also gave him the nickname of The Vampire Killer. Despite the fact he liked the sound of that it was a bit less appealing in this day and age. He wasn't keen on taking the chance on catching HIV or hepatitis. he did think about what they might call him though. The Shadow Killer? The Ghost Killer? The Invisible Killer. He would be happy with any of these names. Notoriety appealed to him.

He decided there and then that he needed to think carefully about his method of disposal. He also needed to think about how he could cleanse any evidence from his crime scene. This was a difficult one as fingerprints could be found even after a surface had been cleaned with bleach. He therefore needed to think out-of-the-box. An entirely new approach would be required. Fortunately, he knew just what he would do. The idea was tucked away in the corner of his mind reserved for the exploration of the perfect murder. Life was good. It was very good.

49

Despite the fact the coveralls could have come from anywhere Shona decided that the local police would have to be interviewed anyway. She needed to know whether they all had alibis for the time that the body was discarded. This would be no mean feat. The highlands and islands covered a large area. She was glad that this little conundrum would be dropped firmly in Neill's lap. The telephone call did not go well.

"You want me to do what? Did I hear right?"

"I'm afraid so. We need to pin down the whereabouts of every police officer within a fifty mile radius."

"I'll need an exact time." Neill's tone was flat. "You do realise that Dundee is a 15 mile radius from us. You'll need to interview all of your guys as well."

"I didn't say you needed to interview anyone. I said find out where they were at 1 a.m. a couple of nights ago."

"That's all is it? That means we need to check all the alibis as well. That will take forever."

"We'd both better hop to it then. Speak soon. Bye." She neatly finished the conversation by abruptly hanging up. She knew how the chief felt.

"She wasn't as cheerful as She sounded on the phone. Neill was right, forever is exactly how long it would take. There were hundreds of officers in Tayside police. She decided that for once she needed some help. She headed towards the chief's office.

"You want to do what?" There was silence for a few minutes and then, "You have come up with some harebrained schemes in your time but this one is a legendary."

"I agree, Sir. However it is necessary. There's no other way around it."

"Leave this with me. I need to speak to the chief constable."

"Thank you, Sir."

"Don't thank me. I'm sure the chief constable will be sacking you. I'm tempted to do so myself. Get out of my office."

Shona was glad to leave. She was hoping the chief constable would come up with something that would take it out of her hands. For once she wasn't even thinking about killing the chief. She actually felt sorry for the poor man.

"And you're still alive to tell the tale," asked Nina.

"Barely. I might just be dead when the chief constable catches up with me."

"How he's going to achieve that wee trick, escapes me. I dinnae even want to think about it," said Peter.

"I'm sure the chief constable has superpowers. He'll get it all sorted with minimum of fuss and maximum efficiency." said Shona.

"It was nice knowing you. I'll start a collection for your leaving present now." Roy was grinning from ear to ear.

"Cheeky beggar. Don't forget I'm still your boss for now."

"I wouldn't have it any other way, Ma'am."

Shona decided to pay Mary a visit. If nothing else she could have a seat for five minutes in Mary's office. Mary was keen to have a break and chat so they settled down on the comfortable sofas.

"Thank goodness for a bit of normality," said Shona.

"If you think this is normal than your life is a tragedy,"

said   Mary.
"My life's a soap opera."

"What can I do for you, Shona?"

"Now that all the body parts have been identified I was wondering if you had any earthly clue what was going on? Have you picked up any evidence from them?"

"The only thing I can tell you is that they had all been frozen. Apart from Lucinda that is."

"I don't suppose the killer had time to freeze Lucinda. She was found pretty soon after she was killed."

"One other thing. These bodies have been chopped up by an expert. They knew exactly what they were doing and where to cut. Lucinda's head, before it was battered, was sliced in just the right place."

"Great. Are you any clearer as to whether they would need to be a surgeon or not?"

"In some ways I'd say yes. But I don't think this has quite got the finesse of an experienced surgeon. Perhaps someone who starting out."

"Maybe someone became a surgeon just so they could learn the skills for this."

"That's some career plan. It takes years to get to the stage where they let you loose with a knife."

"Good point. Who would have the patience or ability to develop this level of skill? I think our boy, or girl I suppose, is escalating which worries me."

"They certainly dumped the last one quickly enough," said Mary.

"I'm fresh out of ideas to stop him. If you have any, now would be the time to chip in."

"Ideas are not my forte. I'm here to deal in the hard facts which are given to me in the shape of a human body."

"And very good at it you are too. I couldn't do the

job without your support and extensive knowledge."

"Away with you. What are you after?"

Laughing, Shona left her to it and returned to her work. If nothing else she was now feeling a bit more cheerful.

Just to prove that CID's work was never done, Shona had a phone call from the desk sergeant.

"I'm sending someone up to see you. Young Brian Gevers is bringing her up as we speak. Her name is Danielle Bellamy.

"OMG." This retort came, as if as one, from a number of positions in the room. "Boys! Bring your jaws up and keep you're fly's zipped."

Even Shona had to agree that the woman was a stunner. All long legs, blond hair and perfect make up she held the room in the palm of her hands.

Not that she should be in that particular room. Shona took charge.

"Please could you come through to an interview room?" She indicated that the woman should follow her and gave the nod to Abigail to do the same. She didn't trust the boys to keep their mind on the interview and away from the woman's anatomy.

She was here to report that her wife was missing. By this point Shona was wondering if someone was out to rid the world of lesbians. After her last case she wouldn't be surprised at anything.

"What was your wife's name, Mrs Bellamy?"

"Carrie. Carrie Bailey-Bellamy. She wanted to keep her name as well as mine."

"How long has your wife been missing?"

"Two days. She went to work two days ago and didn't come home."

"Has your wife ever gone away without telling you before?"

"Never. She's gone off on holiday without me before. She's the outdoors type and I'm not. So we sometimes have separate holidays. We always arrange them in advance though."

"Do you think she could have just gone away from a few days?"

"No. She would've said."

"Was there any indication she was having problems? Had you had any arguments disagreements, anything at all that would have made her go off on her own?"

"Nothing at all. The only holiday we were planning was a round the world trip. We were going to take six months off and go travelling. Together." She emphasised the last word.

"Where did your wife work?"

"She was a lawyer. She worked for a firm in town."

"It wasn't with McClusky and Runcie was it?"

"No, Peverell and Brown." Danielle's look indicated she was a tad puzzled.

Rats, thought Shona. I was just in the mood for a tussle with the battleship and her brother.

"Have you spoken to her friends and family?"

"Yes. No one's seen or heard from her."

"What about the hospitals?"

"I haven't gone that far." The woman's breathing quickened. "Do you think something's happened to her? Do you think she's hurt?"

"We can't speculate at the moment. We will need to investigate. Do you have a photo we can use?"

"I thought you'd ask that. I brought one with me."

The woman in the photo was even more beautiful than the one standing in front of them, if that was possible. What a couple.

"Do you mind if we come and have a look around your house? It might give us a little better perspective on what might have happened."

"I'll let you do anything if it helps you to find Carrie. I'm going crazy without her. Please you've got to find her."

"We will certainly do our very best. You can be certain of that."

"Do you really think it's someone with a vendetta against lesbians?" asked Peter.

"Looks like it."

"At least it's not nuns or vicars."

"Thank heavens for that. I don't think the church would ever forgive us if we started on them again. For once we haven't had any member of the ecclesiastical fraternity involved in this case. I'm sure the chief is delighted."

"Who would you like to go and search the flat?"

"All of us. It will be much quicker." She paused. "No. Leave someone here to phone the hospitals. Grab everyone else and we'll meet at the flat. One seven five two Perth road."

The flat was spacious as an estate agent would say. Shona's take on it was that it was humongous. It was in one of the old brown stone Dundee properties which were originally owned by the mill owners. The floor-to-ceiling bay windows had a view that someone would kill for. Not that that was the best metaphor to use given the circumstances, thought Shona. The flat was beautifully decorated and no expense had been spared.

"My, these girls have taste," said Nina. "What I wouldn't give for an apartment like this."

"You are here to work, Nina, not admire their taste

in curtains. You might want to put some of your efforts into searching the flat."

The decoration fetish came to an end and the work proceeded at a rapid clip. Nothing seemed untoward. Didn't appear to be any of Carrie's clothes missing. The flat was clean but there was no evidence of it having been scrubbed with particular fervour. Forensics threw up nothing unusual, not a single, solitary bloodstain.

"Wherever Mrs Carrie-Bellamy may be, she wasn't bumped off in here," said Shona.

"Do you think this is part of our case?" asked Abigail.

"My gut's are telling me it is."

"Is that not the curry you had last night?" Said Roy.

"Don't give up the day job. The world of comedy isn't quite ready for you yet."

It turned out Carrie Bailley-Bellamy wasn't in any of the hospitals either.

"Do you think it could be something to do with one of the cases she was working on?" asked Peter.

"Could be. It's something we definitely need to look into. I'm off to speak to Peverell and Brown. Let's see what they have to say for themselves."

It turned out that neither Peverell nor Brown could help them. Carrie had been working on nothing more dangerous than the sale of property. In fact it would seem that was pretty much all she ever worked on.

"What a boring way to make a living," said Shona.

"It pays well though by the looks of the flat they live in. You wouldn't get much change out of quarter of a million. Their clothes are designer chic as well."

"Nina! You're obsessed. Never mind how much they're worth, we've a missing women to find."

"Are you sure it's not a missing corpse we're

looking for?"

"I sincerely hope not."

50

Much of the research had been done. It was now time to bring all the threads of his plan together. Piece, by expensive piece, he started to buy all the equipment he would need. Some of it wasn't quite so expensive but to someone with his income it was a large outlay. A few pieces were eye wateringly expensive. Still he only wanted the best. This was not a time to think about saving money with poor tools. So, he went for professional level.

He started small. He still had time to build up the perfect collection. He wanted to have all the necessary equipment before his first kill. But, he also wanted the feel of a knife in his hand. Therefore the first thing he bought was a boning knife. This was closely followed by the purchase of a skinning knife and a meat cleaver. His knife collection was complete when he bought a meat saw and a professional level bone saw. By the time he bought this he was earning enough that the purchase price was a mere bagatelle. Not that it mattered. He would have bought it anyway.

However, he needed more than knives. The whole thing started with the question, how does one dispose of a body? This question still filled both his waking thoughts and his dreams. Buckets and containers were added to his equipment inventory. A steel table suitable for carrying out a post-mortem was harder to find. Still, after a lot of research and a measure of patience, the item was his. He needed this in order to make sure the blood ran into waiting receptacles rather than drip onto the floor. The disposing of the body was always at the forefront of his mind. It was a clandestine deal done on the black market. No questions asked. He wanted no record of the deal. Neither did the seller.

Three glass topped display freezers were purchased and moved into the room he prepared to butcher the carcass. He had to see it as a carcass not a human. Then he obtained numerous yards of thick plastic. A sturdy spade joined the growing pile as he checked the last item from his list.

51

Shona knew she wouldn't be left in peace for very long. The shrill ring of the phone interrupted her reverie. It was the Dunkeld police with news of another body.

"Where is it?"

"It's not quite body. It's almost a body."

"What's it missing?"

"It's head."

"So where is this almost body?"

"Atholl Woods, on the edge of Polney Loch."

He might as well have been speaking Mandarin for all Shona understood. She went to find Peter, the oracle of all things Scottish.

"They're about an hour away near Dunkeld. They're part of the path network of Dunkeld and Birnam. Birnam woods was mentioned in Shakespeare's Macbeth.

"Peter stop wittering. I asked for the location not a lesson in literature."

"I thought you'd be interested because o' your cat."

Shona rolled her eyes, and went to break the news to the chief they were off on another jaunt.

"Inspector, why do you always insist on chasing around the countryside? My fuel bill is higher than that of British Airways."

"Maybe you could claim it back from the other force whose work we seem to be doing?"

"Maybe you could stop telling me how to do my job. I'm perfectly capable of working out the station finances without any help from you."

"Sir, I—"

"That will be all."

She left the office thinking that it might be a good

idea to chop his body into a million tiny pieces. Then she could feed them to the fish in Polney Loch. This thought cheered her all the way to the edge of said loch.

The view was magnificent. Despite the rain, the view through the trees and over the grey, wind whipped loch, took Shona's breath away. She stood transfixed for a few moments, forgetting the seriousness of her visit, and then turned back to the business of the day. The body was that of a woman. That was apparent, as she was naked. This time she hadn't been discarded as much as tucked. Tucked under a bush. Only part of the body could be seen, but it was quite clear that she was missing her head.

"I'd say she's roughly the same age as our other women," said Shona.

"And I'd bet my pension that this is our missing lassie, Carrie Bellamy," said Peter.

"We shouldn't be speculating, but I'd put a fiver on the fact you're right."

"That poor we lassie. She didnae deserve this."

"None of them did, Peter. None of them did." Shona was expecting to see the prints of a couple of wolves or something but there seemed to be a complete lack of wildlife at this scene. She was almost disappointed. Iain was cracking on with the photographs whilst the others patrolled the perimeter looking for clues. Roy was noticeable by his absence as he was back at the station combing through the interweb. His computer wizz kid brain was searching for any possible connection between the women. Apart from the fact that most of them were gay that is. Shona whipped out her iPhone. They'd all been upgraded and she had a top of the range iPhone 6S plus. It was meant to make life easier for them. She dialled Roy's number and when he answered said, "Contact Lucinda St John-

Smith's friends. I want to know if there was any whiff of a rumour that she might be gay."

"I've not found anything that would indicate that so far. In fact quite the opposite."

"Are you saying she was promiscuous?"

"Not promiscuous, as far as I know. But she did have a lot of male friends."

"See what you can find. We'll be back in a couple of hours."

She turned back to the crime scene." Who found her?"

"A courting couple. They've been sent to a bothy to shelter."

"That would have tamed their ardour."

"By the looks of them I don't think their ardour will ever return."

"Seeing a body without a head must have thrown their ardour into the loch. Probably accompanied by the contents of their stomachs."

"I've sent Abigail with them. She's going to take their statement. Then they're going to be carted off in an ambulance to be checked at the local walk-in clinic. The pair of them looked like they were about to gasp their last."

"Any evidence come to light?"

"There are a lot of footprints as you can well imagine," said Iain. "These woods are part of the Dunkeld and Birnam public right-of-way so they're well used."

"Good point. This is going to be fun then," said Shona. "

"It's a bonnie area, Ma'am. It's interesting."

"Maybe we should concentrate on the task at hand. You can tell me all about the area over a glass of whisky in the pub later."

Iain thought it would be circumspect to drop the

matter. "I've got some nice clear casts of the footprints and some of a few partials."

"You never cease to amaze me. Clear prints in this morass of sodden leaves are truly a miracle. Do your best and then we'll hand the whole shebang over to the locals."

Talking of locals a man walked up to Shona and held out his hand. Before he could open his mouth Shona said, "What are you doing strolling around in my crime scene?"

The man dropped his hand. "I'm the local police surgeon. I came to pronounce the body."

"Pronounce the body. A blind man could see from two miles away that the woman is dead. She's missing her head for Pete's sake."

"There's no need to be rude. There are protocols to be followed."

"Well I've already started the investigation. I didn't think I'd have to wait for a doctor."

"Well you should have done. If you're ever in my area again I will expect you to wait."

"Sorry. Will do." Shona couldn't be bothered expending any more energy on the argument. They must pay police surgeons well if they trail into the middle of nowhere to declare a headless corpse as being dead.

She was glad to be back at the office. Beautiful the area may have been, but it was also isolated, cold, wet and windy. Why would anyone want to trail out there to dump a body, she thought? Surely burying them under the patio would be a damn site easier. Why did serial killers make life so difficult for themselves? They certainly did in Dundee that was for sure.

She rang Mary to warn about the headless corpse which was winging its way to her doorstep.

While she was on the phone she decided to clarify something. "Why would a police surgeon come out to declare a headless corpse dead. Surely it's a bit superfluous. I know protocol demand someone with medical training is necessary, but surely under those circumstances?"

"You're right it does need somebody with medical training. But I agree with you under those circumstances most people will take it as read."

"The local police surgeon came out to the middle of nowhere to declare my corpse. He had a wasted journey. One look was all it needed."

"Where were you?"

"Atholl Wood. Why? What difference does that make?"

"That explains it then. It would have been Derek Digby who turned up. He's a miserable old goat and a money grabbing miser. He'd declare one of your missing fingers if he could make a couple of quid."

"You're right. He is miserable, and rude."

"He's been worse since his wife left. Much as I'd love to stand and gossip about Derek all day I've got several Dead bodies awaiting my tender ministrations."

"I've several murders to solve as well."

"Roy what have you got for me?"

"I've been in touch with Lucinda's friends. According to them no sign that she was gay. They've known her since they were at school together and it's been males all the way."

"Could she have been in the closet?"

"I asked that and they said no. Never a whisper of it."

"Has anything come up on either Bertram or Henry?"

"Nothing so far. I'm keeping it to the right side of

the law though. I don't fancy being sued by Henry whether he's innocent or not."

"I agree. Keep it that way. He'd spend his time in chokey thinking up ways to persecute us."

"I've arranged to go out for a drink with him tonight. We got chatting and I told him he could do with a night out. We're going to that new wine bar on the Perth Road," said Roy. "Any chance I could put it down to expenses?"

"Not a chance in hell. Your night out is going to be done on your own shilling."

"It was worth a try." Roy's grin said it all. "I'll try and get to know him a bit better. See if I can get him to loosen up a bit."

"Just be careful, Lone Ranger. He's not thick. It might be better to take Jason along for extra security."

"Nah, I'm good. I don't fancy a night out with Soldier Boy."

"You pair aren't fighting again, are you?" Shona's tone indicated the answer had better be the one she wanted to hear.

"No. We're bosom buddies. I just can't take too much of him at one time."

"Go catch a killer."

She went to release the troops from bondage. "Your loved ones will have your dinner on the table. Off you go and eat it."

"It's no' dinner time, it's tea time," said Peter.

"So I speak English. Get over it." Shona's smile softened the words.

She went to speak to her loved one to find out what they were going to do for tea. Douglas may be exasperating her at present but she still had a feeling of great excitement at the thought of seeing him.

52

All the pieces were now in place, or at least most of them. All that remained was for him to set up a location where he could put his research into practice. This was not as easy as it seemed. He needed the perfect venue. He spent many hours looking at properties all over Scotland. Each one was dismissed as not having exactly the right qualities that were necessary for him to do a good job. No, not a good job, a perfect job.

Location also played a large part in his plan coming to fruition. It needed to be somewhere with easy reach to much of the rest of Scotland. Good road links were essential. As was the fact that he needed easy access to remote areas. He pored over maps and decided on the perfect location.

Some final preparation and he would be ready. Anticipation swelled within him so deeply and fully he imagined it would burst out of him. He managed to keep it under control and carried out his 'normal' life.

53

Hammering on the door woke her from a deep sleep. She stumbled to the door and yanked it open. "What? Stop that infernal racket."

Douglas stood there. "You're okay. Thank goodness you're okay." He pulled her into a hug that would have made a bear feel feeble.

"Of course I'm okay. What are you going on about?"

"When you didn't turn up at work we assumed the worst."

"It's not time for..." She looked at her watch. Ten to Ten. "Oh my giddy aunt. Make coffee." She flew in the direction of the bedroom.

There were cheers when she staggered into the station, clutching a travel mug of double strength fully loaded caffiene.

"Glad you could make it, Ma'am. Have you gone part time?"

"Shut it, Roy, or you'll be sent to Traffic for a couple of months."

"What were you up to last night then?" asked Nina.

"None of your business. Get some work done."

She quaffed her coffee like a woman who was going to the gallows and then went to face the chief.

"I don't know whether to be angry or relieved. Buy yourself an alarm clock woman."

"Sorry, Sir." She seemed to say that a lot where the chief was concerned. "It won't happen again."

"I know it won't. The policemen guarding your flats will be knocking your door at a reasonable time each morning."

"I thought you might call the Rottweilers off."

"Why would I do that? I ordered them to be there. They will stay until I say otherwise."

"Yes, Sir." She wished she could throw the chief in a ring with a pack of rabid Rottweilers. They'd polish him off nicely and leave some other poor soul alone.

Thoughts of rabid Rottweilers were not moving her case forward. A bit of news that Roy brought her moved it forward a few inches.

"Henry St. John-Smith has had a vasectomy."

"So he couldn't be the father of the baby that Lucinda was carrying? Good work, Roy."

She phoned Mary. "Could you take a tissue sample from Lucinda St John-Smith's unborn baby?"

Mary, on the ball as always, knew immediately what the issue might be.

"Paternity testing?"

"Got it in one. Looks like Lucinda was playing an away match."

"That lot have got you with the football talk."

"I'm absorbing it by osmosis. They're all obsessed, including Nina. Abigail's the only one with one iota of sense."

"I'll send the sample off within the hour. I'll get them to fast track it through the system. You're still looking at about seventy two hours as it's for forensic reasons."

"I know. Better to get it done properly though. St John-Smith will have it thrown out before we get to court if we even think about doing otherwise."

"Roy you and I are off to visit your mate Henry. You should be chums after last night and he might be a bit more open. Plus, you're the one with the technical knowledge if he asks awkward questions about where we found this info."

On the way to Henry's luxury crib she asked Roy how the previous night out with Henry had gone?

"Did he give you anything."

"Apart from about twenty free drinks and a hangover, nothing. He's pretty generous with his dosh."

"He didn't let anything slip at all?"

"Not even a sniff. I know I'd had a lot to drink but I was still compos mentis."

"Roy! You're not still drunk are you?"

"No. My mate's a medic. He sorted me out."

"What did he do? On second thoughts I don't want to know."

"Best not. It may have been a little on the grey side of the law."

"Thanks for agreeing to talk to us, Henry." Shona started out like a lamb. She'd leave the lion stuff for later.

"Can I get you a drink?"

They both declined and Shona said, "Some new information has come to light."

"About my wife? Have you found her killer?"

"No. We need to ask you some personal questions."

Henry was suddenly all lawyer in contrast to his previous affable host persona.

"There is nothing in my personal life you need to know about."

"I'm sure, given your occupation, you will be aware that we need to know everything about you. Is it true you have had a vasectomy?"

"I don't wish to answer that."

"Fine you'll answer it in court." The lion was making itself known sooner than Shona expected. "I don't have time for this. Answer the damn question. It's simple enough."

Henry smiled and said, "You look lovely when you're riled."

"What? Are you coming on to me when I'm investigating your wife's murder?"

"I am merely paying you a compliment. Yes."

"Yes what?" Shona felt like she'd dropped down the rabbit hole.

"Yes. I've had a vasectomy. How did you find out?" The smile was gone and his eyes narrowed. Shona was intrigued that they stayed as bright as ever.

She looked at Roy who said, "Your wife was talking about it on Facebook a few years back."

"If she wasn't dead already, I'd kill her myself. Who talks about deeply personal stuff like that on Facebook?"

"Apparently your wife did. It seems he wasn't that keen on the idea. Talk of murder is not the best move in here Henry."

"It's just an expression. I don't know why she was saying that. We both agreed that we didn't want children."

"How come you were so excited about the fact you were having a baby then?"

"I got used to the idea. I'd grown a bit. I'm a bit more mature. It was the right time I suppose."

"The burning question is, how was your wife able to get pregnant if you'd had a Vasectomy? Did you have a reversal?"

Henry looked Shona straight in the eye and said, "I haven't had a reversal. It obviously failed."

"I had a look before we came and the failure rate is around nought point one five percent. With odds like that the chance of your wife getting pregnant was pretty slim."

"But there was still a chance. It would seem that

we were in the less than one percent that it happened to. We couldn't have been happier about it."

"Did you not for one minute think it could have been somebody else's baby?"

"Of course I did. But my wife assured me that it was mine and I believed her."

"You realise that we will have to do DNA testing on the foetus?"

"You cannot do DNA testing on a foetus without permission."

"Absolutely right. But given that we are investigating a murder we have a warrant that says we can."

"That's" a gross invasion of my privacy."

"I'm sure you will realise that my right to investigate your wife's murder, trumps your right to privacy."

"I'm not going to say anything else without a lawyer present."

"You are a freaking lawyer. Surely you don't need another one cluttering the place up."

"If you want to ask me any more questions, then you can do so in the interview room with my lawyer present."

"Who's your lawyer?"

"Margaret McCluskey."

"How did I know that was going to be an answer?"

Shona didn't have the energy to deal with both Henry and Margaret in one room. She decided they would investigate a bit further before she arranged that particular interview. She updated the others on what had gone down.

"Would it be worth investigating whether Henry had a private DNA test done?" asked Nina.

"Yep. Although I'm not exactly sure how he would

have managed that little feat without his wife knowing and consenting. More than consenting in fact. She would also have had to comply."

"Not now. You can do it from a blood sample now," said Iain.

"How would he get enough blood for a sample."

"Henry's probably got an IQ that's off the scale. I'm sure he could work it out," said Nina.

"Right you've convinced me. Roy—"

"I'm on it," he said as he headed from the room. If that information is to be found then Roy was the man to find it.

Less than an hour later he was back. "There's not a lab in the country which has run that test."

"How did you manage to get that information so quickly?"

"Do you want the truth or the doctored version?"

"I don't want any version. Suffice to say I'm impressed."

"So it's not looking like he bumped his wife off because she was knocked up by another man" said Roy.

"As always your turn of phrase never ceases to amaze me. However, it is likely."

"That'll be a dead end then?"

"Not necessarily, Roy. Not necessarily."

A few hours later Roy came up trumps again. He was certainly the man of the moment in this case.

"It would appear that Bertram has been married previously. He lived in Malaysia, and his Malaysian wife died under a mysterious circumstances."

"Good work, Roy. You'll be getting a gold medal by the end of this case."

"I'd rather have a couple of thousand quid bonus in the old pay packet."

"You're chancing your mitt. You've as much

chance of that as the snowman has of remaining upright in hell."

Roy laughed and handed over a sheet of paper. "Here's the contact details for the police in Kuala Lumpur where he lived."

"You might just get that bonus yet."

The Malaysian police were extremely helpful. They informed her they would fish out all the relevant documentation and skype her later in the day. Whilst she was in a hiatus wondering what the next surprise would be, the DNA results came back on their headless corpse. This particular piece of information was not a surprise as the woman was the missing Carrie Bellamy.

Yet again Shona found herself knocking on the front door of the flat in the Perth Road. Once inside and sitting down she said, "I'm sorry to have to tell you, Danielle but Carrie is dead. We have found her body."

The woman stared, swallowed and then started to rock. It was then that the high pitched keening began.

"Nooooooo. Nooooooo." Sobs wracked her body as she continued to rock.

This continued and Shona was beginning to get worried. "Get a Doctor here," she said to Abigail. "Then make her a cup of tea with lots of sugar in it."

Abigail jumped to do her bidding and Shona sat with her arm around Danielle. The tea appeared within five minutes.

"It's herbal tea. That's all they've got. They had almond milk in the fridge but I didn't think I ought to use it."

Shona took the cup and held it up to Danielle's chattering teeth. The woman was now shaking so much she wouldn't have been capable of holding it herself. She took a sip and choked. Shona put the cup down and waited for the doctor.

The doctor immediately phoned for an ambulance and then injected Danielle with some substance that would calm her down. Within ten minutes she had been carted off to A&E.

"Go with her, Nina. Interview her the minute she's coherent. By her reaction I don't think she's got anything to do with it but we'd better be certain. Be gentle with the poor woman."

When she got back to the salt mines she poured fresh, steaming hot coffee into a mug and inhaled the aroma. She took it back to her office but before she could take one restorative sip a small figure appeared in her office.

"Hiya, Shona. We've come to see you."

"I can see that. Where's your brother?"

Rory walked in and gave her a cheery wave. He was too busy listening to his music to communicate otherwise.

"Daddy has a big meeting with the biggest man here he said. Can we stay here with you?"

"There's not much room, Alice. Why don't I take you both along to the squad room. I'm sure they'll provide cake and entertainment."

"Will uncle Peter be there?"

"Yes he will." Peter wasn't really their uncle but the kids loved him. It probably had something to do with the copious amounts of cake and sweets he fed them.

Rory pronounced himself starving so Peter dragged them off to the canteen. They would be even more spoilt by Doreen and Annie. The kids didn't just belong to the procurator fiscal, they belonged to the whole station.

The Kuala Lumpur police skyped her back. "We've pulled the files and it seems you've nothing to worry about. Mr Peirs was married to a Malaysian National. She was stabbed to death and we did investigate her husband."

"It sounds to me like we should be worried."

"Not at all. The husband was elsewhere when it happened. He had gone down to Singapore on business. A couple of years ago we caught her killer. The man owned up when he was arrested for killing another woman. A tourist."

"Thanks for your help."

Another lead that had fizzled out. Bertram did seem to have a rather unfortunate track record with wives. She jolly well hoped he didn't get hitched again.

54

With the next development Shona was eternally grateful the children were no longer in her office. Or anywhere near the squad room for that matter. Iain quietly entered the room and closed the door. He was pale and looked like he was having difficulty keeping it together.

"Sit down. What's wrong?" Worry added a sharp edge to Shona's tone.

"I don't know how to tell you this, Ma'am." He swallowed, and then swallowed again.

Whatever it was it must be bad, thought Shona. Iain usually took everything in his stride.

"Take it easy but I need to know. I can't do anything to help without you telling me what the problem is."

"The white coveralls were found in a bin. Miles out in the country. My oppo sent them on to me."

"Why would that upset you. Hang on, why didn't I know about this development?"

"I wanted to make sure they were relevant before I brought it to you."

"It's still no excuse." She gritted her teeth and breathed deeply. "Go on."

"They were filthy so I wasn't sure I'd get anything useful from them."

"Never mind that…" She stopped and lowered her voice. Ian was obviously distraught. Her voice softened. "What's upsetting you? Where are the coveralls?"

"In my lab. I thought I'd test them for blood. There was blood. Anya Peirs' and Daisy Murray's."

"What? On the same coveralls?"

Iain's head hung even lower, if that were possible.

There were fingerprints in the blood and DNA inside the suit. They belonged to..."

"Iain, whatever it is you found it can't be that bad. Who did they belong to?"

"Roy. They belonged to Roy."

"Roy? Roy McGregor. Our Roy?" Shona couldn't get her head around this.

"Yes, Ma'am. I couldn't believe it myself so tested it several times."

Shona sat back and stared at him. "Are you absolutely positive."

"Yes, Ma'am. It would stand up in court."

She went pale. "That's not reassuring me, Iain. Go back to the lab and do not say a word to anyone. Bring everything to me and I will lock all the results away."

"You're not going to cover this up are you, Ma'am?"

"Of course not. I'm going to speak to the chief."

The chief slumped in his chair and scratched his head. Raised eyebrows signified his disbelief.

"This had better not be a wind up, Inspector."

"I wish it was. I'm afraid this is deadly serious, Sir."

The chief closed his eyes. Shona waited. After a few seconds he opened his eyes again and said, "You will have to investigate this. Do nothing until I give you the green light. I need to update the superintendent and the chief constable. Say nothing to anyone."

Her heart heavy Shona returned to her office.

The children were carted off by their father. Shona managed to hold it together long enough to hug them and wave them a cheery goodbye. Then she barricaded herself in her office with the excuse she had a mountain of paperwork to catch up on.

"The chief will have my hide if I don't catch up. He's on one of his efficiency drives."

That was the truth but she certainly wouldn't be doing any. Before she returned to the office she went to speak to Iain.

"I want you to look at every single fibre of that suit. Examine every blood spatter to see if Roy could have been set up."

"I already have, Ma'am. I don't see how. There's not a fingerprint on there that doesn't belong to him."

"Do it again. Then after that do it again if you have to. When you're finished we'll get it looked at by someone independent. If you need me then ring me. I've told the team that I'm unavailable."

It was a couple of hours before the chief came to find her. By this point she had made some inroads on the paperwork mountain. It was the only distraction therapy she could think of. The chief's news was not good.

"You need to interview and arrest him, Shona," he said in a gentle voice. This was the first sign of compassion she had ever seen from the chief. "Would you like me to do it?"

"Thank you, Sir, but I'd better do it."

"The chief constable is on his way. He's in Glasgow at the moment but will be here in a couple of hours."

Before she could arrest Roy she had to brief the team. This was not going to be easy.

55

All his research was now complete. It was time. He no longer needed to read books or gain new knowledge. All the knowledge he needed was now inside his head. Squirrelled away in a secret vault known only to him. It was now time to unlock the vault and put that knowledge to the test.

He chose the woman at random. He wasn't sure what it was about her that caught his eye. Was it the swing of her hips? The evocative tilt to her head? The voluptuous body? The sound of her joyous laughter? maybe it was the sum of all of these. He just knew that she was the one. This would be his first run in real life. He had gone over everything in his head a million times.

First he had to get to know his subject. He watched her from afar and within weeks knew everything about her from her favourite clothes to the exact colour of paint on her spanking new Ford Focus car. Ask him her favourite food or drink, that was easy - chicken with lemongrass and chilli sauce with special fried rice, and blue WKD to drink. What time she got up for work - 6 a.m. How often she dyed her hair - monthly, and always a different colour. For months he stalked her and she, totally unaware. he even said good morning to her a couple of times. She had no clue as to his intentions. This was a good thing. Her last months on earth would not be filled with terror. Her last minutes would be.

Her car was parked up a dark side street whilst she went to her night class. French as she was going on holiday to Nice. She parked it there to avoid paying for parking. It was a few minute job for him to disable her car. At the end of the class she got into the car and switched it on. Nothing happened. It was then he made his move. A stranger with a dazzling smile who offered to help. He pulled the tools from his own car. They included a rag and a bottle of fluid. Within seconds she was also disabled.

56

Telling the team was even harder than she imagined. She called them all to the briefing room but left Roy doing a detailed search on the Internet. This was nothing new as this was often the case. She told them what had happened and waited. There was silence which no one was willing to break.

After what felt like hours but was, in reality, minutes, Peter said, "Why? What possible motive would he have?"

"I can't get my head around it, " added Nina. "I mean, Roy's a bit of a prat but he's not a killer."

"No way. There's no way he would do that." Jason, Roy's most unlikely ally was almost shouting.

"Jason, Keep your voice down. I know you're shocked but there's no need to act like a child. I don't want Roy to hear"

Silence fell once more and was broken by Shona. "I will have to interview him. Peter, I would like you to be in there with me."

Peter looked like she'd kicked him but said, "Of course. I understand."

She gave him an almost imperceptible nod. She was glad she had Peter on her side.

"Roy, I need you to come to the interview room with Peter and me."

"Why? Do you need some muscle?"

"Something like that."

When they entered interview room Roy asked, "Where's the prisoner?"

"I'm sorry Alisdair but we have to interview you."

At the use of his real name Roy swivelled towards her. "What. Why?"

"Sit down, please."

Peter switched on the recording equipment.

"Interview with Alisdair McGregor...." She finished the remainder of the preliminaries.

"What's going on? I haven't done anything. You know I haven't."

"Where were you on the nights of..." She reeled off the dates when Lucinda and Carrie's bodies were discarded in the woods.

It was as though a lightbulb went off in Roy's head. His usually deep voice rose until it was almost a treble. 'What? You don't think I had something to do with those women?"

"Mr McGregor please stop shouting."

"Shouting? No wonder I'm shouting. How could you do this?"

Shona remained resolute. She had to. This was possibly the single most difficult task she had performed in her career so far.

She showed him photographs of the blood stained coveralls. "Your fingerprints are all over these. How do you explain this?'

"I have no idea. Please you've got to believe me."

"That is somewhat difficult to believe in light of the evidence. It looks like your DNA may also be inside the garment."

Roy's eyes dulled. He had come to a sudden realisation of how much trouble he was in.

Shona paused, took a deep breath, and resigned herself. "Alisdair McGregor, I am arresting you for the murders of Anya Peirs, Daisy Murray, Trisha Leyland, Lucinda St. John-Smith and Carrie Bellamy. You do not have to say anything but anything you do say maybe taken down and used in evidence against you." Roy's shoulders slumped. He stood, as Peter gently took him by the arm. Shona turned, tears in her eyes, and walked out of the door.

"Peter, get him a lawyer. A good one," she called after them.

57

It was easy to get her inside the house. The electric entrance gates opened at the touch of a button, as did the garage door. He merely lifted her from the car and straight in to his specially prepared room. Laying her down on the autopsy table he gazed in wonder. He allowed himself a few minutes of pleasure, then got to work.

First he opened a vial of a deadly medication. This had been the hardest part of the plan to bring to fruition. Fortunately, by the time he had come this far, one could buy anything from the Internet. Part of his research and planning had been to work out how not to leave a trail. This would not form part of his own digital footprint. Using a syringe and needle he drew the drug from the vial. He then applied a tourniquet to the arm of the comatose woman. He expertly injected the contents of the syringe. A slight whimper as the needle pierced the skin, but the woman was soon dead. She did not suffer. Making sure she was dead, he then picked up the first instrument. That first slice was exquisite pleasure.

He picked up the finely honed and sharpened butchers saw. Within minutes the first limb was expertly severed. A cow could be butchered in twelve minutes. His first human carcass was slower. He wanted to savour the experience. The feel of flesh on his hands the sound of the rivers of blood flowing. When the body had been skilfully butchered each piece was placed carefully in a freezer in the correct section. His collection had begun.

58

Shona realised that they would have to search Roy's house. As he lived with his parents, this was not going to be an easy task. She could not even warn them as this could allow them to dispose of any evidence. Not that she thought they would. She had met Roy's parents, who were a lovely couple. Their only flaw, as far as she could see, was that they loved their son to the point of obsession.

Warrant in hand they walked up the gravel path of a garden, which was a riot of bright plants. It was a delightful splash of colour in the midst of the dank autumn day. Not that Shona was able to appreciate the colour. Her heart heavy she knocked on the door. Her action was about to ruin the lives of another two individuals. Mrs McGregor welcomed them in with open arms.

"Where's Alisdair?" Then realisation dawned. "Has he had an accident? Is he dead?"

Shona was quick to reassure her. "No. No. Nothing like that. Nothing has happened to him."

Shona's next words killed the woman's relieved look. She was asked to sit in the car and Brian Gevers sat with her. Shona had brought him along as she needed her full team to perform the search. This was done efficiently but with the utmost speed. The only thing they found was a t-shirt with a small amount of blood on the sleeve. His personal computer and laptop were also taken as evidence. Mrs McGregor was accompanied back to the house just as her husband drove up the road like the hounds of hell were following him. He abandoned the car and flew into the house.

Shona realised that no one had eaten for some time. "Do you want to grab something to eat?"

"I couldn't eat if you gave me a million pounds. I feel like I'm gonna throw up," said Jason.

The rest of the team agreed.

The chief constable had arrived and Shona was asked to bring him up to date. He took notes and when she'd finished said, "Well done Shona. This must be almost impossible for you. If you need any help at all then please let me know."

The chief took over. "This may be even more difficult than arresting DC McGregor. We will need to hold a press conference."

"Sir, you can't do that to Roy's parents."

"We have no choice. If we don't, we take the chance of being accused of a cover up."

Shona hung her head.

The chief constable said, "I will do it, but you will need to be there. If you are not it implies you were complicit in his actions."

Shona squared her shoulders. She had a job to do and she would do it to the best of her ability. "I'll be there, Sir. What time would you like me to arrange it for?"

The press conference was as bad as Shona imagined. The room was packed as all the local papers for a fifty mile radius, every national paper, and both the BBC and STV was represented. The chief constable remained both calm and professional. Shona could see why he had reached the highest rank in the Scottish police.

"Police Scotland can tell you that they have a

suspect in custody for the recent killings which have taken place in Tayside. This suspect is DC Alisdair McGregor of Dundee CID."

There was an audible gasp, which rippled around the room. Even the hard bitten reporters were shocked.

"The public can be assured that the suspect will be investigated using the full force of the law. That will be all. There will be no questions at this time."

With this he moved away from the mike. The crowd went wild as the saying goes. Shona could now understand the saying, baying for blood. Despite the head honcho's exhortation that there would be no questions they were shouted from everywhere. The residents of the Tower of Babal would have felt right at home in this room, thought Shona.

"Who on earth are we going to get to look at Roy's computers? He's probably got them locked up tighter than a Scotsman's wallet," said Shona

"You might want to think about what you're saying, Ma'am. We're all Scottish, including you," said Nina.

"Sorry." Everyone was tetchy so Shona made a mental note to steer clear of any witticisms until further notice. "Any bright ideas on a computer search?"

"I think Brian Gevers might be good on computers," said Jason. I've heard him and Roy talk some weird sort of language. The only word I understood was Gigabytes."

"Fine, I'll ask his Sergeant if we can borrow him until further notice. I'm off to speak to Roy. Peter, come with me."

Roy was sitting on the edge of his bunk and had the look of a condemned man.

"How are you, Roy?"

His look said are you for real? He didn't articulate it. In fact he couldn't utter a word.

"I'm sorry, but we need your personal computer passwords."

He sat and contemplated the question for a minute and then, "Give me a pen and notebook." He wrote something down. "This is the URL and password for a password vault. Go there and you'll have access to all my passwords."

"Roy, the Sheriff has agreed you can stay here. You're not being moved to a general prison."

Roy sighed and his shoulders visibly relaxed. "Thank you."

Both he and Shona knew what would happen to a rogue copper in prison.

59

A few long days later the investigation was going nowhere. They were no further forwards with the case than they were in flying to Jupiter.

"Brian, has your computer search thrown anything up?" He was sitting at a table in the corner of the room. Shona couldn't bring herself to give him Roy's desk.

"Apart from the fact he's heavily into women and gaming. No."

"Women? There's no porn on that computer is there?"

"No, Ma'am. Just scantily clad women. I think the computers need to be looked at by a digital forensics expert though."

"You're right. That's my next step. You'd better go back to uniform."

She was arranging the transfer of the computers to digital forensics when Iain came bounding in.

"You're looking remarkably chirpy for someone who condemned Roy to a life sentence a couple of days ago.

"I have some more results back from the main forensics lab at Rushton Court. It's good news. At least I think it's good news."

"In the name of all that's Holy tell me what your wittering on about. I take it by your expression that it's something that helps Roy?"

"Yes, Ma'am."

"Roy could have done twenty years before you get around to telling me."

"I found some more DNA and a partial on the inside of the coveralls."

"And you didn't think to tell me this?"

"Didn't want to get everyone's hopes up. Anyway I sent it off to Rushton court and the results have just come in."

"So you said. What are they? I swear I'm going to be the next member of the station to kill someone."

"Your predecessor got there before you."

"What are you talking about? Never mind. What were the freaking results?"

"Oh, sorry. The DNA and partial were from Henry St. John-Smith."

"I knew there was something up with that man. I didn't think he was our murderer though." She stopped and thought for a moment. "How the hell did he set Roy up to take the fall."

"Can we go and let Roy out?"

"No. I want to lull Henry into a false sense of security. When you're not in the briefing room you'll look as sombre as ever. No one tells Roy under any circumstances."

He looked shocked but agreed.

When she outlined her plan to the chief he agreed it was the right course of action. The team on the other hand were not convinced..

"That's inhumane," said Nina.

"Much as I feel like locking him up at times, you can't leave the poor lad languishing," said Nina.

"It is a wee bit cruel, but I understand where your coming from," added Peter.

Jason was the one lone dissenting voice. "Best place for him," he said with a huge grin on his face.

"How did Henry get the evidence from Roy?" asked Iain.

"They were out drinking one night. He got Roy drunk and I suspect he also drugged him."

"He had this well planned out. I can't believe I

went out with him. Evil—"

Nina, I know you're shocked but mind your language.

"Sorry."

"We're not discussing your love life, Nina. Now, when you are all out of this room you act like Roy is still guilty. Do I make myself clear? If Roy gets a whiff of this I'm sacking the lot of you."

There were agreements all round.

"Peter and Jason. Go and fetch Henry in. Don't use handcuffs. We don't want him to know we're on to him. Try and do it without that. He should be at work."

She turned to the remainder of the team. "Grab your coats, we're going to search Henry's house again.

60

He had bought a small cottage in a rural area. A very rural area. This gave him a place to relax, a bolthole if he was in trouble, and an excuse for regular travel. This brought him full circle, back to his original question. Simple. One merely chopped them up and disposed of them in a million different places. Eking it out so the police did not have a clue. The only thing that he needed to be careful off were CCTV cameras. This was easy enough in the country. Not a camera in sight. Unless it belonged to a twitcher of course. He thought this idea was inspired. Brilliant.

So he drove up that road listening to his music, with the human leg rolling around in the boot. He took the sturdy spade out of the boot and buried his prize. It would never see the light of day again.

Then, he closed the boot, got back into the car and continued his journey. It was time for a few days of relaxation before he started again.

61

The search of Henry's house continued as before. Not a thing to be found. His car was there which was strange. Iain crawled under it to look for anything untoward and found it was resting on a burlap sack. As he moved it over he noticed something.

"There's a trapdoor under here."

They bumped the car out of the way then smashed their way through the locked trapdoor. Judicious use of the battering ram did the trick. They stood stock still as they reached the bottom of the stairs. A huge room, stretched before them. It was filled with bookcases, fridges and an autopsy table.

"No one go any further. Iain, take photos. Nina get Sgt Muir here now."

Once the photo's had been taken she and Iain put overshoes on and examined the fridges, which were packed with body parts.

"Ma'am, you'll want to look at this," said Iain.

The long wall was end to end corkboards full of photographs. There were neatly squared off sections full of photographs of women. There were also detailed notes.

"This is research on the women. He must have been stalking them for months. She reached the end and started to shake. The last section was full of photographs of her."

"Shona are you okay?" Nina hurried over ignoring Shona's order to stay put. She took one look at the wall and said. "He's been stalking you. You were to be his latest victim."

Shona found a shaky voice from somewhere. "I probably would have been if it wasn't for the chief and the Rottweillers."

"You seem to be missing a prisoner," said Shona when they returned. Peter was busy making phone calls. He stopped and answered her

"We can't find him."

"What do you mean you can't find him? You lot seem to make a habit of returning to the station empty handed."

"He's gone off to his cottage in Arrochar."

"Where's that?"

"Near Inveraray."

Some more of the puzzle fell into place. "Lets go. Stab vest and guns for everyone"

Once suitably kitted out they were out the door and into their cars. Brian Gevers had joined them since they were one man down. For once it wasn't only Shona who drove like a stock car driver.

Despite the need for speed she drove carefully. These were narrow winding roads through the highlands. Torrential rain and winding roads made the journey treacherous. The rain lessened off as they approached Henry's remote cottage. Tucked in the shelter of a craggy hill and surrounded by the ubiquitous Scottish Pine, it stood well back from the road. Shona stopped them before they arrived. They were rendezvousing with the local Bobbies who were lending support. There was a back entrance so she asked Highlands and Islands to cover that. This was the most sensible move as the Dundonian squad had no clue where they were going.

They approached the house slowly. As they did, a silver car shot past them.

"That's a Porsche Cayenne," said Jason, a touch of wonder in his voice. "You wouldn't get much change out of a hundred and fifty thousand buying that."

"Never mind the car. That's henry St. John-Smith driving it." She was busy turning their far inferior Peugot police car.

As she started the chase she radioed the details of the car through to the others. She cranked the car up to top speed. "Did you see which way he turned?"

"Left at the end of the road," said Nina. "He's heading north."

Shona took her word for it. She screamed left round the corner and the chase began.

"Speeding car on the high road. I think it's him," said Jason. He was peering into his iPhone. Take a right in 600 yards." The thrill of the chase had taken Jason's mind off the fact that Shona's driving usually had him a quivering wreck.

Shona expertly manoeuvred the car and they were on their way once more. The chase continued. It would be getting smaller as Highlands and Islands were setting up Roadblocks.

They were just about managing to keep the car in sight when it disappeared. Completely.

Shona screeched to a halt. "Where did he go?"

"There has to be a hidden road," said Peter. "There's a lot o' that round here. They were used for smuggling whisky in the olden days."

Shona slowly reversed the car. The others got out and had a look.

"Here," shouted Peter.

They leapt back in the car and Shona pushed it past overhanging tree branches. She'd probably scratched the car beyond all recognition but she'd worry about that later.

The car bounced along the rutted road. Road was a misnomer. She'd have called it a path.

"This must have played havoc with that Porche's

suspension, " said Jason.

"Will you shut up about the frigging Porsche. Who care's if it's damaged."

"But—"

"Jason!"

He wisely shut his mouth. They found the car sooner than they thought. Abandoned with its doors open. Jason looked like a kid in a sweet shop. They left the police car, slowly. They looked around and proceeded at a snails pace. Henry was nowhere to be seen.

"If this is a whisky road he's probably hiding in an old still." said Peter.

"Should be easy enough to find him then," said Shona.

"Are you having a laugh?" said Nina. "They were built to hide from the exciseman.

"You'd have a better chance o' finding a nuclear bunker," added Peter.

"So where do we go?"

"Follow me." Peter took the lead and Shona was happy to comply.

They moved inch by painful inch, scanning every inch of the area. They had fanned out in pairs as the others knew what they were looking for. A movement stopped Shona and Peter dead. Their heartbeats quickened as they held their breath. A small doe burst from the trees and bolted past them. They continued their search. Peter stopped and whispered in her ear. "Over there." He pointed to a barely visible opening.

"How are we going to get him out of there?"

"We're going to smoke him out," said Jason. The others had arrived at the same spot.

"With what?" asked Shona. We didn't exactly come prepared."

"I did. He pulled a smoke grenade from his

pocket."

"Where..." Then she remembered that he and the civilian who issued weapons were old Army muckers. "You haven't brought a rifle with you?" she asked. Jason always seemed to manage to get a rifle when everyone else had a pistol.

"No."

"I'll be speaking to you later. Go ahead. Use the grenade."

Jason pulled the pin and the accurately thrown grenade sailed through the opening of the still. Jason's Army training brought with it some impressive skills.

A billow of smoke erupted from the hole and Henry staggered out, coughing fit to bust a vital organ. He mustered up enough energy to throw a meat cleaver in their general direction. It mostly missed but the handle managed to batter into Jason's chest. He was protected by the stab vest but still grunted. The others rushed up and soon had Henry handcuffed.

"Henry St. John-Smith you are under arrest for the murders of Anya Peirs, Daisy Murray, Trisha Leyland, Lucinda St. John-Smith and Carrie Bellamy. You do not have to say anything but anything you do say may be taken down and used in evidence against you."

They threw him in the back of the police car and used some handcuffs on his ankles for good measure. They didn't want him lashing out with his feet and causing a crash. It was a long trip back to the nick.

62

When they got back to the station and charged Henry with murder Shona was free to release Roy. He bounded out of the cell and said, " I could kiss you on the mouth."

"Cut it big mouth. You'll regret anything you say. You didn't think I'd let you take the rap for this did you?"

"I thought my life was over."

"Don't be such a sook. I needed to lull the real killer into a false sense of security. You were a sprat to catch a mackerel."

"How did he get my DNA?"

"That'll teach you to go out drinking with a serial killing lawyer."

"I missed the chase. That's the best bit."

"I'd ask you to come and help interview him if I didn't think we'd end up in the deepest mire. Given the man framed you we better keep you apart. I don't fancy rearresting you for murder."

"So I don't get to go anywhere near him then."

"Not on your nellie. You need to stay as far away from him as possible." She took one look at Roy's face and added, "I mean it Roy. The case will be thrown out of court if you even whisper one word to him."

"I pinkie promise."

She knew Roy would keep his word.

"Go home and get yourself sorted out. We'll see you tomorrow."

"Did you notice his eye colour has changed?" asked Abigail.

"It looks like the blue eyes were contact lenses. I

thought they were a bit bright to be real."

Henry was back to his usual persona of full on charm. It was difficult to imagine him as a serial killer.

"Mr St John-Smith why did you kill all those women?"

"Because I wanted to. It was an experiment."

"An experiment? You did all this as an experiment. Into what?"

"How I could kill someone and dispose of the body."

"You killed five women just to see how you could get rid of them?"

"No. I killed nine women."

"Nine? You killed nine in total? Who are the others?"

"Do you think I'm stupid enough to tell you lot that?"

Shona decided to deal with that later. She sat back in her chair. She needed to recover from the shock.

"I thought you had a vendetta against lesbians."

"That was just a side line. I agreed with Bertram I would kill his wife. He disapproved of her lifestyle choice."

"You did what?" Shona's voice had risen by several decibels.

"Bertram needed his wife killed and I agreed to do it." He looked at her as if she were simple.

She darted from the room leaving Henry in the charge of a couple of coppers and Jason.

"Peter, go and arrest Bertram Peirs for incitement to commit murder,"

"What?" He was speaking to the air. Shona had bolted back to her prisoner.

"How did you know Bertram Peirs?"

"We went to the same boarding school for about six months. We bumped into each other again about a year ago. He told me he was having trouble with his wife."

"Take this bag of crap back to his cell."

Shona updated the chief whilst she waited for the others to return with Bertram.

"Well done Shona. I see you managed to do it without anyone getting injured this time. You're improving."

As always the chief couldn't give her a compliment without the implied insult being attached.

They returned empty handed as per usual.

"I jolly well hope that Bertram Peirs is in a cell waiting for me to interview him?"

She knew her answer before Peter even spoke.

"No, Ma'am. He's gone. Bertram Peirs has flown the nest."

"Did you search his house?'

"Of course we did." Peter's look said she wouldn't live that question down for some months. "His clothes were gone. From the empty safe we saw I'd say his passport and money flew with him."

"Was there anything else?"

"He left an envelope with your name on it."

Shona took the envelope, slit it open and pulled out a thick sheet of cream writing paper. She read the words aloud.

Inspector,

If you are reading this then you will realise what I have done. Although mine was not the hand that killed my wife, I was complicit in the act. Do I regret what I did? No. Not for one minute. She deserved to die. A woman should be subservient to her husband. My wife did not display those traits. Therefore, there was no other course of action. I am long gone now, and you will not find me. I bid you adieu.

Bertram Peirs.

"Wouldn't divorce have been a better option?" asked Abigail.

"It certainly would. Especially since he will not escape the consequences of his actions. We are going to spend as long as it takes hunting him down. Hell hath no fury like an Inspector scorned."

WENDY H. JONES

Wendy H. Jones lives in Dundee, Scotland, and her police procedural series featuring Detective Inspector Shona McKenzie, is set in Dundee.

Wendy, who is a committed Christian, has led a varied and adventurous life. Her love for adventure led to her joining the Royal Navy to undertake nurse training. After six years in the Navy she joined the Army where she served as an Officer for a further 17 years. This took her all over the world including the Middle East and the Far East. Much of her spare time is now spent travelling around the UK, and lands much further afield.

As well as nursing Wendy also worked for many years in Academia. This led to publication in academic textbooks and journals. Killer's Cross is the third book in the Shona McKenzie series.

THE DI SHONA McKENZIE MYSTERIES

Killer's Countdown
Killer's Craft
Killer's Cross
Killer's Cut

FIND OUT MORE

Website: http://www.wendyhjones.com

Full list of links: http://about.me/WendyHJones

Twitter: https://twitter.com/WendyHJones

Photographs of the places mentioned in the book can be found at: http://www.pinterest.com/wjones64/my-dundee/

Made in the USA
Charleston, SC
13 April 2016